THE LITTLE GUN

The smallest man. The fastest draw.
The deadliest vengeance.

With a giant horse at his side and a quick draw deadlier than any gunslinger, Jedidiah carves his name into frontier history. But vengeance has a price— and for Little Gun, justice may cost more than his soul.

Terry Godfrey

The Little Gun

Copyright 2025 by Terry Godfrey

Printed in the United States of America

For more information or to book an event contact:

Email: indianheadrock@currently.com

Cover design by: Joseph Maddox

ISBN paperback: 978-1-965142-72-1

ISBN hardback: 978-1-965142-73-8

First Edition October 2025

QUILL HAWK PUBLISHING

Edmond, OK

This is a fictional story, and the main character did not exist. There was a dwarf in the Wild West show, but that person was a lady. This story is fiction for the entertainment purposes of the reader only. Though Morgan horses are not true draft horses, many were used during that time to pull plows and wagons. They were a larger breed of horses of the time.

Contents

Chapter 1: Hard Knocks

Jedidiah was born in the mountain country of southwestern Missouri during the fall of 1859. His mother died giving him birth, and his father died a few years later. He was raised by Jessica, his sister who was a comforting and compassionate caregiver to a troubled young boy. She was only nine years old when their father died, leaving her alone to care for a four-year-old brother. Jedidiah did not grow at a normal rate like most boys. His smallness worried their father, who had lost two children, both at childbirth, between Jessica and Jedidiah. Losing two babies and his wife facilitated their father's demise, for he just gave up on living.

By the time Jedidiah was five they had very little left but the run-down shack at the edge of the small town. Jessica left school to work early in the morning, cleaning the saloon and then later the hotel. Jessica barely made enough money to buy them food. By the time her clothes wore out she was able to wear her mother's. They were a little large on her, but she made them work.

Jessica put Jedidiah in school to learn to read, write, and add. That was when his troubles began. He had not grown much and was smaller than all the kids in school. Jedidiah walked to school to hear the sound of laughter. Tim and three of the older boys came from around a tree in front of the school. Tim said, "Hey Shorty, did your mother really kill herself after giving birth to you?" The others would laugh and push him down. Jedidiah would return home to their tiny shack with red eyes and dirty clothes. Jessica would clean him up and tell him that he knew he was a good boy. At only fourteen years old, she worked hard every day. At the end of her workday the owner said to her, "You are a hard worker young lady. Your brother is lucky to have you to care for him." The hotel owner was also pleased, but his new wife took over the cleaning. Jessica asked around the town for more work without any luck. The owner of the saloon offered her a job serving drinks. With some reservations, she took the job. Most of the men that came in knew she was there to serve drinks and did not bother her.

Jedidiah missed her not being home in the evenings but knew she was working to buy food for them to eat. He played in the backyard after school once he finished his chores. They had a few chickens and an old milk cow from before their father died. Each morning before school, Jedidiah gathered the eggs and milked the cow while Jessica fixed breakfast. She would take the milk and eggs into town to sell them. Any spare change went into a bag and was hidden behind a loose rock on the fireplace.

Since Jessica came in early in the mornings to clean and then stayed to serve drinks, the owner allowed her to leave work early in the evening. He had other girls working in the evening. The arrangement allowed Jessica to get home and fix supper for herself and her little brother. Jessica was growing taller and beginning to look like a beautiful young lady. The majority of the men knew her and treated her with respect, unlike the girls who worked late at night. However, some of the men in the saloon took notice of her.

Few people ever saw Jedidiah except the school kids, as he stayed away from the people as much as possible due to the relentless teasing of his small stature. Bitterness came as he grew older without growing in size. He did not hate other people; he just did not want to have anything to do with them. His sister Jessica was his whole life; if anything happened to her, he did not know what he would do.

One evening, Jessica came home late to fix their supper. She had been crying as he could see her eyes were red. Jedidiah did not ask what was wrong, thinking that she would tell him when she was ready. While placing the food on the table, she told him that a man had grabbed her in the saloon. The other men pushed him back and made him leave. The owner told him not to come back. "You are picked on like me," asked Jedidiah?

"Yes, I am picked on but not like you. Some men are pigs," Jessica said. "There are a lot of decent men around though."

"It is like the kids," Jedidiah said. "There are some mean ones, but most are okay. Good kids just won't take up for anybody else."

"Most kids have not learned compassion yet," Jessica stated.

They finished their supper and prepared for bed. Jessica slept in their parent's old room while Jedidiah had the small loft to himself. It was a very small space that looked like a storage area. They had shared the space till their father died. Now it was all Jedidiah's, which was a good thing as there wouldn't be enough room for Jessica. She had grown to twice the size of Jedidiah. Each time he had trouble at school, he wanted to quit and go to work.

"Where do you think you would be able to work?" Jessica would ask him. That would leave Jedidiah silent and thinking.

Jedidiah started walking up into the mountains alone after school. He always liked being alone, out in the woods, with nothing but his father's old knife as a companion. It was nearly as long as his arm. When he went out into the woods and mountains he practiced wielding it like a sword. One afternoon, he was higher on Baldy Mountain than he had ever been, practicing with his knife, when he heard a voice.

"If you ain't careful, you'll hurt yourself with that pig sticker." the voice proclaimed. An old man was watching him. "Shit, you're older than I thought."

"You want to make something of it?" Jedidiah said as he puffed out his chest.

"Naw, but I guess you can handle that Arkansas toothpick alright."

"I have been handling it for most of my life."

"What's ya doing up here all alone?" the old man asked.

"I just like to get away on my own," Jedidiah said. "Most people pick on me and call me names, so I stay away from them."

The old man told him that was a good way to stay out of trouble, but most youngens didn't understand that. Jedidiah told him that he had been trying to find a job, but

nobody wanted to hire a dwarf. He also told him he was
tired of school because everyone there picked on him.

The old man asked, "Ya mind skinning pelts and
helping me cure them? I'll share the profit from the sales if
ya help." Jedidiah told him he would love to do that. "Well,
I'm William. I have a trap line all across these mountains."

It was a long line that took most of the day to run,
since game had become scarce. All the people moving in
drove the game out. There weren't many trappers around
anymore for that reason, and most had moved further west.
William told Jedidiah he was too old to move again. This
was his home, and he would die right here.

Jedidiah helped him skin out what game he had,
showing him what he could do. Later that night when
Jessica came home, he told her he had a job. Jessica sat
listening to him nodding her head in understanding. She
wanted to give him the opportunity to have his say before
she replied. "I can do this and not be bothered with others,"
Jedidiah said. "I will leave for work early each morning
and come home late." A benefit of this was he had fewer
encounters with others. "I will not be going back to
school," he proclaimed.

The job with William worked out great for Jedidiah.
William spent most of the time running his trap lines.
Jedidiah skinned the game and stretched the hides out to
cure. Late one afternoon they sat together talking and
William told him that he had a son, but he ran off to St.
Louis to find a job. William had hoped that his son would
take over one day, but now it would be Jedidiah's if he
wanted it. Once the hides were cured, William would take
them to the city and sell them. He would then come back

with the money and split it evenly with Jedidiah. With this job he was now making almost as much as Jessica, working two jobs.

William asked Jedidiah, "Have ya ever shot a gun?"

"No," Jedidiah told him. "I don't have one and never had a chance to shoot one either."

William pulled out an old pistol and showed Jedidiah how to use it safely. He allowed the young boy to shoot it. Soon, Jedidiah was very prolific with the pistol. Willaim let him try a rifle one afternoon and he was very accurate with the rifle. They had become friends and worked well together. William was pleased with the way Jedidiah worked and had a growing respect for him.

Jedidiah started placing money in the bag behind the loose rock on their fireplace. The bag was getting fairly full with a substantial amount of money. Jessica stayed later and later at the saloon. She never did anything but clean and serve drinks. There was one man, however, whom she spent more and more time talking to.

The saloon owner noticed but did not say anything about it until one morning, he mentioned, "I hope you have a chance with that young man." The young man was a shop keepers' son and stood to inherit the store one day. "He's good and kind."

Jedidiah went to the mountain to work one morning. He was supposed to meet William there and collect his share of the sale. He had not worked the last two days since William was away to the city selling pelts. Jedidiah got to the camp where he cleaned the hides and William was not there. He waited and waited but William did not show up. Finally, he left and went back home. Jessica came home to check on him as her boss had told her she needed to. "Jedidiah, William was found on the road between here and the city," Jessica said. "He's dead. There wasn't any money on him." It was apparent William had been killed for his earnings. " I have to go back to work. Are you going to be okay?"

"Who would do this to him? He was the only person other than you that was ever nice to me. William was teaching me more than I ever learned in school." Jedidiah then told her he was fine, and she should go back to work.

Later that day, Jessica returned to work and two of the evening girls did not show up. The owner asked her if she would mind working late. He told her she did not have to do anything but serve drinks. There was one other girl there who was a favorite of the men. She could handle them alright. Jessica was not happy about it but agreed to work late. She kept thinking about Jedidiah and was worried about him but thought he would be okay.

Late into the night, four men whom she had never seen before, came into the saloon. They spent money wildly. The other girl was with them and going from one to the other. They sat at a table close to the bar, but Jessica did not have to serve them as the other girl was staying with them. Not long after, though, they started noticing Jessica. One of them slapped her ass each time she walked by. They became more aggressive. Alice the other girl was all over them and getting paid for her attention, but Jessica did not want that kind of money. Harry the owner noticed all this and the roughness of the four men. It was getting late, and most of the locals had left. Harry caught Jessica and told her she could go home for the night. She collected her earnings and left out the back door.

One of the men watched Jessica leaving out the back and nudged the others telling them it was time to leave. As they went out the front, he told them his plan. The men caught Jessica in the alley of the next block going out of town. Two of them held her down while one took her. One man riffled through her belongings in search of her pay. They each traded places and took turns till each had his way with her. The second man was the roughest; he slapped her around as he took her. By the time they were through with Jessica, she was barely alive.

Jessica started to crawl away, but a tall skinny man grabbed her and beat her. She ripped his face with her fingernails. He hit her repeatedly till she dropped dead.

Hours later, a drunk stumbled over her. He was nearly passing out but became fully aware when he saw what lay on the ground before him. He reported the crime to the sheriff, saying, "I found a young woman's body lying in the alley." Sometime later, the sheriff visited Jedidiah with the horrific news.

"There were four men in the saloon harassing your sister," the sheriff said. "My posse and I are organizing to find them." The owner of the saloon had given him a pretty good description of the men. One was short and stocky. The second was average height and heavy set, with a knife scar on his left cheek. The third was a little over average height and average build. The fourth was tall and very skinny. He doubted that they would be able to catch them in the dark before they reached one of the borders. They were close to the Arkansas border, not far from the Kansas border or from Oklahoma territory either. Jedidiah wanted to go with them, but the sheriff would not allow it.

Jedidiah did not cry; he sat in the small shack and got mad. Never had he hated anyone till now. He thought about his sister and how she had taken care of him for longer than his parents had. One way or another he would get those men. He vowed he would get them all even if it took his whole life to do so.

Late the next day, the sheriff and his posse came back without finding anyone. They found signs that the gang had gone west and were probably in Kansas. The sheriff told Jedidiah that he was certain these same men killed and robbed the old trapper. Some of the money they had spent in the saloon was earmarked. Jedidiah told the sheriff that the old man had been earmarking the money that he paid him with. The sheriff also told him that Jessica must have scratched up one of the men pretty bad. She had a lot of flesh under her fingernails.

Jedidiah made the arrangements for his sister to be buried next to their parents. After the funeral, he went back up the mountain and began running the trapper's line. He had talked with the man at the freight office in town about handling the pelts. The man told him he would ship them for him and give him the money once it was paid. Like the old man William, Jedidiah would run the lines and then skin and cure the hides by himself. With the first pay he got from the sale of pelts, he went to the mercantile and bought the finest colt pistol they had. He also bought a quick draw holster.

For months, Jedidiah worked the trap lines and practiced with his pistol and getting very fast. Jedidiah decided he needed a horse. It seemed that everyone around was riding what they now called cow ponies. There was a horse he wanted at a nearby farm. They raised horses called Morgans. He had walked by the fence many times and made friends with one of the stallions by feeding the horse carrots or apples. Jedidiah would whistle to call the stallion, then give him a treat. " I'm going to call you Goliath," Jedidiah declared. Once he was sure he had enough money to buy the horse, he knocked on the farmhouse door.

The farmer answered and laughed at him for wanting to buy a Morgan horse. A boy who had teased him in school was the son of the farmer and one that laughed at him. Jedidiah showed him his money and asked, "How much do you want for that brown stud with four white stockings?' The man told him a price that was a little high, but Jedidiah accepted with stipulations. "With a price that high, though, you have to provide a saddle and all the rigging.

The man's mouth dropped open as Jedidiah counted out the cash.

Chapter 2: The Hunt Begins

Jedidiah continued to trap and sell his hides, riding into town atop his trusted steed, Goliath. He also kept practicing with his pistol. He now practiced as much from horseback as standing. He wanted Goliath to stand steady when or if he had to shoot from his back. Everyone in town shook their heads when they saw this guy less than four feet tall, packing a fast gun, riding a giant stallion into town. The boys who used to tease him now stayed away from him. Word had gotten around about how fast he was with that six shooter.

One day six months later, while he was in town selling his hides, the sheriff came up to Jedidiah and said, "I have some news about the four men. They shot a man outside of Kansas City and robbed him. They left him for dead, but he made it into town to describe the men who robbed him. There is no doubt that it was the same four men."

"Thank you, Sheriff. Can you help me sell my house?" Jedidiah asked. "I'll be leaving soon for Kansas."

"Lad, you shouldn't be going after them outlaws. I have 'Wanted' posters made up on them and have wired them out to every lawman west of here," the sheriff claimed.

" I'm going after them and I ain't stopping till all four are in the grave," Jedidiah promised. "It doesn't matter if I put them there or if they hang. I'll see them dead."

The sheriff set up an auction for estate sales on back taxes. It was not so troublesome selling for someone wanting it sold. The house was neither big nor finely furnished, but it would be worth something. Perhaps one of the girls working in the saloon would want to buy it. That gave the sheriff an idea. He asked Jedidiah if he would not rather lease it out, just in case he wanted to return some day. The sheriff said he would oversee it for him and either wire him the money or put it up till he returned. Jedidiah thought about that for a while and agreed. There might come a time when he would need more money, he could wire for it if that time came. Jedidiah made the deal with the sheriff and told him to keep twenty-five percent for himself, for handling the property. The sheriff told him that it was more than fair and that he would take good care of it.

Jedidiah purchased the supplies he needed for the road. The way he would travel was not as wild as it used to be. There were many outlaws, though. Towns and cities were sparsely spaced, but he would only be a few days from the next one. Being totally alone now for almost a year he knew he could take care of himself. He had heard enough about the world to know not to show his money. The money he had he placed small amounts in different places among his things. He was cautious to place the money in socks, sleeping roll and saddle bag all of no interest to others.

A day later, Jedidiah mounted Goliath and rode out of the town. Two of the saloon girls moved into his house

and were very thankful to him for it. They both knew
Jessica and respected her. They promise to keep the house
clean and in good repair. He told them that he had given the
sheriff authority to use some of his money to pay for
lumber or anything that was needed for repairs. Jedidiah
rode away from the only home he ever knew at the age of
eleven with one mission in mind–to find the men who
raped and killed his sister.

Jedidiah headed northwest toward Kansas City.
There was a large town straight north which the old man
had been returning from before he was robbed and killed by
those bandits. Jedidiah took a more direct route toward his
objective, hoping to cut a few days off his journey. As
night drew close, he looked for a place to camp for the
night. He rounded a bend and saw a fire in the distance.
Intending to avoid encountering others he rode out and
around the campsite. It was late before he circled around
and back to the creek bed. By this time, he was over a mile
from the other camp. He watered Goliath and fed him
before eating something himself. "I won't be making a fire
tonight," he muttered, not wishing to show he was there.

Jedidiah woke well before dawn and made a small
fire under a large pine tree. The wood he used was old and
very dry, giving off very little smoke. In the early morning
dawn, the smoke would not show, nor would the small fire.
The fire kept burning just long enough to make a little
coffee and cook breakfast. He fed Goliath before he ate his
breakfast and then he mounted and moved on. Realizing the
difficulty of mounting such a large animal with his small
statue, Jedidiah trained Goliath to kneel on his front knees
and allow him to climb up his neck. A rope ladder he made

was tied to the saddle on the left side. He could climb the ladder, pull it up after himself, and then tie it off.

The next day and night were uneventful for Jedidiah. He was able to build a fire and rest peacefully. Jedidiah placed the saddle near the fire and lay on it with a blanket over him. Keeping his pistol near his hand, under the blanket through the night, ready for a fight at any time became a habit. Jedidiah had become very high strung, always ready to strike. Goliath would awaken him if anything approached during the night as his hearing was better and he was more alert for danger.

One day while he was running the traps, he walked upon a copperhead snake. He pulled his pistol and shot its head off while it was midway through its strike. Jedediah was prepared to face down the outlaws that had killed his sister.

The next night he was getting closer to the twin cities of Kansas City–each city was on either side of the Missouri river, one in Kansas and the other in Missouri. There were a few small towns outside the cities on both sides. Spending one more night on the trail, he then went into a small town. He made a camp right at dusk with a small fire to cook under a pine. While the food was heating up, he fed Goliath and gave him water.

Perhaps due to his size, Goliath was extremely tolerant of him. The longer they were together, the more Jedidiah was trusting and dependent on his four-legged companion. Jedidiah put the fire out and was getting ready for bed when Goliath whined. Placing his things on the saddle and covering them with a blanket he acted as if he didn't notice anything odd. Then he stepped back into the shadows next to a large tree.

Two men walked slowly into his camp. They pointed guns at his blanket and shouted, "Get up." One of them shouted again and kicked the blanket. It flew off the saddle to reveal no one was there. They both turned looking for him. Jedidiah told them softly from the shadows to drop their guns. They did not and as he stepped out around the tree, they both shot above his head. Before either could pull the hammer back for a second shot, he killed them both. He shot the one closest to him in the head and the other in the heart. Their single-action pistols were no match for Jedidiah's new, double-action colt. He did not have to pull the hammer before firing again as they did. And because they both shot at him first, he did not feel any remorse about killing them.

The next morning Jedidiah found their horses and tied them to Goliath. As he could not put their bodies on their horses, he made a travois, rolled them onto the A-frame structure, and tied it to one of their horses. He rode like this into the nearest town. Once there, he went straight to the sheriff's office and told him what had happened. The sheriff took one look at them and knew who they were.

"These two brothers had gone bad," the sheriff said. "I have warrants on them and there's a small bounty." The sheriff looked at the bullet wounds and then checked their guns. Seeing that everything matched what Jedidiah told him, he accepted it as fact. The sheriff then asked, "How'd you outshoot the two of them?"

Jedidiah told him, "They shot over my head, and I was fast enough to shoot them both before they could get off a second shot."

Jedidiah collected the bounty then asked the sheriff if he had heard anything about four outlaws. He described them and retold the story of how they raped and killed his sister. "I'm on their trail."

" I heard they had some trouble on the other side of Kansas City but that's all I know," the sheriff said. "I've seen the 'Wanted' posters on them, though, and as a matter of fact, I've got the posters hanging on my wall."

Jedidiah then asked about Kansas City and what to expect. The sheriff told him it was a prospering city now with law and accommodating for most people. Jedidiah told him, "Obviously I am not like most people." The sheriff laughed and told him that as long as he did not cause trouble, they would not bother him.

Jedidiah asked, "Is there a clean place in town that would accept me for the night?"

" There's a boarding house that is nice," the sheriff offered. "I'll vouch for you. You'll be able to get a peaceful night's rest with no trouble."

Jedidiah took Goliath to the stable and bedded him down for the night. It was a short walk down the street to the boarding house where he checked in with the widow who ran it. He rested well and got up just in time for breakfast. As he walked down the stairs, he realized it was the smell of coffee and bacon cooking that had awakened him. As he ate, the widow and two other men stared at him. When he looked up, they looked away. Jedidiah was used to that and did not pay them any attention.

One man, though, finally asked, "You are the man that brought in the two Bradford brothers, aren't you?"

"Yes, I am," Jedidiah stated as he moved his right hand down his leg, ready to draw his gun.

The man told him, "Thank you. Those guys stole from us all. They were bad men."

Jedidiah was surprised that they were not blaming him or making fun of him but thanking him for killing those outlaws. This was a new experience for Jedidiah. The emotions they expressed gave him surprise and delight. Shortly after breakfast he went to the stable and mounted Goliath. He rode out toward Kansas City. Knowing that he would have to go to the ferry and pay to cross, Jedidiah had the money in hand. The man at breakfast told him the price and procedure for crossing the river. From there he would be in Kansas City, Kansas, by early afternoon.

After crossing the river, Jedidiah rode into Kansas City, Kansas. A few people stopped and stared, but most seemed not to care. Jedidiah was amazed at the size of the city. He thought he would just ride to the jail and ask for the sheriff. This was very different. He rode for some time and finally asked someone where the sheriff's office was.

Arriving at the sheriff's office, still perching on Goliath, he inquired with the deputy in front of the building. The deputy dropped his mouth open and told him he would go get the sheriff.

The deputy ran into the office, "Sheriff you need to go out front right away. There is something out thar you just gotta see." The sheriff wanted to know why he should rush outside for anybody. The deputy said, "you wouldn't believe me unless you saw it for yourself." The sheriff of

Kansas City stepped out of his office. This was something that he normally would not do. The deputy told him he needed to be a trusted and long-time friend. As the sheriff stepped out of the office, his eyes went wide. He wasn't sure what he was seeing. Before him was a giant horse with the smallest man he had ever seen atop of him. The man looked him straight in the eye and told him he was looking for four men who were seen in the area.

"They had robbed a man near here," Jedidiah said. "They also raped and killed my sister and killed my good friend back in Missouri."

The sheriff told Jedidiah he knew of the men he was asking about but had no idea where they were at the time. After the robbery southwest of Kansas City he had sent out a posse looking for them but did not find anything. " I heard they were traveling west toward Dodge City." the sheriff said.

Jedidiah thanked the sheriff. "Say, is there a good place to spend the night and put up my horse?"

The sheriff was happy to accommodate and told him about some good places. Jedidiah put Goliath up for the night in the best stable that had been suggested to him. He then went to a good place nearby to spend the night himself. The next morning after breakfast, Jedediah met up with the sheriff at the stable. The sheriff asked him about the men he had killed and about the four men he had asked about. Jedidiah told him all about the two men that tried to rob him. Then he told the sheriff that the four men he was looking for, had raped and killed his sister and killed his friend. He told the sheriff that he was going to track them down and see that they either hung or died by his hand. The sheriff told him that the warrant for them now had a bounty on it which stated dead or alive. If he was chasing them and had to kill them, it would be considered legal. He further explained that a trial had been held back in Missouri which convicted them to murder. Jedidiah thanked the sheriff and told him he was heading west.

As Jedidiah parted with the sheriff, a strange man followed him unbeknownst to Jedidiah. The man had watched him from the corner of a building. Jedidiah was getting Goliath out of his stall when the man confronted him. "You killed my brother." The hair bristled up on Jedidiah's neck as he prepared to draw.

"Drop your gun and come with me," a familiar voice commanded.

The sheriff came in behind the man with a shotgun and poked him in the back. "Jedidiah, you can go. I'll be keeping this one in my cell for a while to cool off. Perhaps I have papers on him too," the sheriff said.

"Goodbye, Sheriff, and thanks again," Jedidiah stated, and he rode out of the stable.

"No problem. I saw this fellow come out of the shadows and follow you so I thought I might see what he was up to. So long and good luck finding those men," said the sheriff.

Chapter 3: First to Die

Jedidiah rode till just before dark. After riding the last couple hours across the open prairie, he began looking for a place to camp. There were few trees around, and he could see for miles. Upon seeing a long line of trees in the distance, he thought *there's probably a stream or river there.* Finding water, he decided he could make his camp near a stream. As he approached the tree line, he looked up and down the horizon for any sign of others or a campfire. Once he entered the trees, he stopped and looked back across the prairie to see if he was being followed. Not seeing any indication of others around, he eased his way to a fair-sized creek in the middle of the tree line. He had to ride upstream a short distance before he spotted a good campsite. It was on the opposite side of the creek, which he preferred. The old man trapper had told him many times it was best to cross the stream when you got there if you could. That way, if it rained heavily overnight, you wouldn't have to wait for the flow to go down to cross.

Jedidiah let Goliath drink water from the creek as they crossed. He led him to a fallen log which he stood on then removed the saddle and rubbed the giant horse down while he ate the oats that Jedidiah brought along. Once Goliath was cared for, he set up his camp and prepared his evening meal. "Goliath if you hear or smell anything strange let know boy." After eating, Jedidiah curled up in his blanket laying against his saddle. Soon he was fast asleep.

Jedidiah awakened with the dawn of the day. He rode out of the trees into a wide-open prairie and scrutinized the area in front of him, before leaving the shadows of the timber behind.

Along his journey, he saw deer grazing. On the trail he enjoyed the morning air and watched rabbits and turkey move along the prairie. Surely, he would be able to get a shot at a turkey or other small game for his dinner.

Riding quietly all day, from time to time, he thought he could hear something in the distance. By evening, he was sure that he was hearing something south of him and it was getting closer. He crossed a couple of small streams, but it was too early to stop. As he came into another opening again, he could hear something closer to his south. From his height atop Goliath, he could see a straight line paralleling his trail. Then he spotted a group of men working along that line. The way they were working, Jedidiah was certain they were building a railway. It became clear he had been riding along a railroad, albeit some distance away.

He came to a small stream that turned in the same direction he was going. Jedidiah veered his path to travel along the opposite side of the stream from the railroad. After a short distance, the stream joined a river on his left with the view of the railroad not far past it. The river ran right next to the railroad. The sun was setting, and he looked for a place to camp. He decided to go right along the river for a while before making camp. He also needed to cross the river before dark. Just before sunset the river curved and he found a good location to camp for the night, without having to cross. Jedidiah made his camp, taking precautions not to show signs of smoke or fire.

In the morning, Jedidiah had multiple smoke trails over the tree line. Jedediah concluded the smoke trails were several breakfast fires along the railroad tracks. From what he could see, the railroad was going to run along the river. The workers' fires seemed to be about a half mile away. Looking around he spotted a tree taller than all the rest. He was certain that he could climb it. From high up in the tree, Jedidiah was able to see the railroad and the men working. They were building a railway bridge over the river. The river went south from where the stream joined it. In the other direction which the river came from, it snaked around going away from the railway and coming back to it. He was glad he hadn't crossed the river the night before. If he went straight on, he would leave the river but come back to it a couple more times before midday. From there he would have to decide which way his trail would go.

Jedidiah rode Goliath slightly northwest for three hours. Twice the river swung back to his path, and he rode alongside it. Well before noon, the river turned back south, and as far as he could see, it didn't return. He turned Goliath south at the edge of the timber, which followed the river. Less than a mile later, he came up on a roadbed for the new train track. Men were there working on the beginnings of another train bridge. They were also building a water tower for the train. Others were working on a building next to the area that had been worked up for the tracks. A short distance away were several tents and a couple of other buildings being constructed. Jedidiah rode into the camp with his hand near his pistol.

As Jedidiah rode up, men stopped their work to look at him. A few laughed while some stood with their mouths gaping wide open. None of the men had seen a sight like this. He was three feet eleven inches tall and rode a large horse that was fifteen hands high. At his side was a special-made Colt 32-20 double action pistol. It had a four-and-a-half-inch barrel and was smaller than most. It was an 1875 model–a small handgun with a common caliber. He could have had a smaller gun, but it would require an uncommon caliber, which would be harder to find ammunition.

There were two men standing in front of a building under construction. Jedidiah rode right up to them, asking if anyone had seen four men going west and described the men he was after. He showed them the "Wanted" poster on the men. They asked him if he was a bounty hunter and he told them no; they had raped and killed his sister. One of the men told him he had seen them two days before, out on the prairie as he was hunting game. They were going southwest toward Emporia. Jedidiah told them good day as he rode out towards the southwest.

Jedidiah watched behind him for an hour as he rode. Minutes before dark he found a place to cross and made his camp on the westward side along a creek. Finding a level place under a large oak tree a few feet above the creek bed he made his camp. After he had watered, fed, and brushed Goliath down, he built up a campfire to cook the rabbit he had shot on the other side of the creek. He had skinned it before making the crossing. He slept well that night.

Jedidiah figured he was two days behind the men that had killed his sister. If he traveled hard, he might catch up with them in Emporia. He rose early, ate a cold breakfast as he fed and prepared Goliath for a long day, and didn't even bother fixing any coffee. Jedidiah rode through till late that night. He was sure that sometime tomorrow he would be in Emporia and hopefully, be able to point out the four outlaws to the local law.

Anxious about what tomorrow might bring, Jedidiah slept restlessly and woke early. He made a quick fire with dry twigs and took care of Goliath while his coffee brewed. Before dawn he ate and was saddled, riding toward Emporia. He had spent the night along the north side of a river which ran west then east. After three hours of riding, the river turned to the northwest. Jedidiah looked for a likely crossing. Goliath took to the river and crossed with him. During the day they crossed four small creeks before coming to another river around midafternoon. Trusting Goliath, Jedidiah walked him northwest along the river looking for a crossing. Sure enough, the Morgan horse turned into the river at a location that was a likely crossing. As they exited the trees along the west side of the river, Jedidiah could see the town in the distance.

It was an hour and a half later that Jediah rode into Emporia. He had ridden wide around the town to approach from the west with the sun low in the sky. The sun shone just above his head as he rode into the town, giving him a perfect view of the street and everyone on it. Anyone looking toward him would be blinded by the sun.

****

Jake, Lester, Brody, and George were sitting at a table near the back wall of the saloon. Brody, the tall skinny one, was sporting a scar along his left cheek where the girl had scratched him. Her fingernails had dug deep into his flesh, and it had become infected. It took months for the wound to heal. Jake told Brody to go across the street and check on their horses. The blacksmith was supposed to finish shoeing the horses today and Jake was eager to head west. Jake figured on cutting some of the herds coming up from Texas. He was also making plans to rob the cattle buyers that were sure to be arriving to meet those herds. Brody stopped at the door and looked back, saying, "That damn Bill Cody is still out there watching for us."

Jake told him, "Let me worry about Cody. Just go check on the horses."

Brody stepped out on the street and started across it. He looked right at Bill Cody, who was watching him. Bill then turned his gaze down the street to the west. Brody was in the middle of the street and turned to look west. A large form moved towards him about seventy yards away. Whoever it was, came right out of the late afternoon sun.

Jedidiah couldn't believe it. Walking right out in front of him was a tall, skinny man with a scar just like a scratch mark. He stopped Goliath and said, "Do you remember the girl that clawed your face?"

"Yeah, that bitch left me scared."

"She was my sister, and you killed her. Drop your gun, and I'll walk you to the sheriff."

Brody said, "Go to hell," as he reached for his gun. Brody's gun went up less than forty-five degrees before he dropped dead in the street.

Bill pulled his gun and told the newcomer to watch the saloon, as there were three more in there that were friends of this one.

With the sound of gunfire, George looked out and saw Brody dead in the street. He could also see Bill Cody across the street, gun in hand. George told the others, and they all slipped out the back door.

Bill Cody, aka Buffalo Bill, stood in amazement as Jedidiah climbed down off his large horse. On the street, Jedidiah was just over waist high to Buffalo Bill, who had seen Jedidiah draw after Brody pulled his pistol and still beat him. The bullet hit Brody square between the eyes, dropping him dead where he stood.

"I offered to take him to the sheriff's office," Jedidiah stated.

"I heard that, and I'll state it was a fair fight," Buffalo Bill said.

"I'm going in after the other three," Jedidiah said. "I have papers on them for killing my sister and my partner." As he walked into the saloon, he saw it was empty except for the bartender. The bar keeper told him the men left out the back door, right after the gun fight. He went after them but saw nothing. Jedidiah went back out onto the street and asked Buffalo Bill where the sheriff's office was.

"I'll walk you over and introduce him to you," Buffalo. Bill said. He told the sheriff what happened, corroborating on Jedidiah's story. Jedidiah showed the sheriff the papers on the four men and told him to have the bounty on Brody sent to the sheriff back home.

It was dark before he finished with the sheriff and Buffalo Bill. Jedidiah asked about a place to eat and sleep for the night. He placed Goliath in the stable with hay and grain. Buffalo Bill invited him to supper at the saloon. "They fix a good steak there, and I would like to talk more with you." Over supper, Buffalo Bill told him that he was looking to put together a wild west show and was looking for a fast gun like him.

Jedediah asked, "Why, do you want a little man with a fast gun? I'm not interested. Besides, I'm going after the other three men. I will not stop till all of them have been hung or I've killed them."

Buffalo Bill wished him luck. "But if you finish your task and want the job, it will be waiting for you." They ate their meal and finished the conversation.

Jedidiah went to bed to get a good night's sleep. The next morning, the sheriff and Buffalo Bill Cody came in and sat by him as he ate breakfast.

"Those three men slipped back into town late last night and got their horses," the sheriff said. "They left going west according to the bartender. He saw them riding out as he was closing up and cleaning the place. I thought it was unusual for a group to leave at that time."

Jedidiah told them, "Word is they are headed to Dodge."

The sheriff said, "I'll wire the Dodge marshal and let him know they are heading his way. Tell him yer on their trail, too." The sheriff agreed to make sure the "Wanted" posters were sent forward as well.

Jedidiah asked about the country between here and Dodge. The sheriff told him it was over two hundred miles, mostly prairie. There was a large town on the way called Hutchinson; he could ask about the men there. He also told him that it got drier with every mile west. He would be able to find water in most of the creeks and rivers, but some may be dry. Before riding out, Jedidiah stocked up on supplies and bought a couple more canteens, filling them all up.

It would take him a week, maybe more, to get to Hutchinson, and at least another week more to get to Dodge. From here on west there were fewer people and towns.

” The towns get increasingly rough the further west you go, too,” Buffalo Bill added. “The exception is Dodge. My friend, Wyatt Earp, just cleaned up the town.”

The railway was on its way to Dodge, and they were getting ready for the cattlemen to drive their stock there. Hundreds of men were working to build the rail across Kansas, all the way out to Dodge.

Chapter 4: Hutchinson

Jedidiah rode out of Emporia on his way to Dodge via Hutchinson. Little did he know that the three killers were a mere five miles ahead of him. They had ridden out of town for a couple of miles and slept for a short time till dawn before moving west.

Jake had them following the construction of the railroad. He was looking for an opportunity to rob a railway payroll. The three stopped a little before sunset at a railroad camp. The workers were not unaccustomed to evening visitors. Although rare, riders along the prairie would stop at a camp to share tales, food, and water. Jake, George, and Lester stopped just outside the camp and called in, "Hello in the camp."

A foreman answered with, "Who are you and what's yer business?"

"Just three travelers looking for a cup of coffee and maybe some vittles," Jake answered.

They were invited in along with some food and coffee. Around the campfire, George asked if anyone was interested in a poker game. He was met with several no's, and one man stated it was two days till the pay came through and everyone was broke. George looked at Jake who nodded his head. They were asking such questions hoping to learn the pay schedule. George put his card deck away, stating that it was too bad. Another man offered that the payroll was supposed to come in with the next supply wagon in a couple of days. George told them they would be far west of there by then. When someone asked where they were headed, Jake quickly told him they were just going west. He told them they were looking for a good way to make their fortune. The foreman offered them a job. Jake told him no; if the workers' money was all gone before the next payday, it wasn't the kind of situation they wanted. He then told them they would be moving on at dawn the next morning.

That night, Jedidiah was only three miles away to the northeast. He was avoiding railroad construction. The old trapper had taught him how to make a camp with a fire which wouldn't be seen. Jedidiah used dry wood to make a small fire under a tall full tree. What little smoke there was would disperse through the tree as it passed. His camp was on a bench just above a flowing creek. He had dragged a log to the open side of the fire to block any glow. Here he fixed a pot of coffee and cooked his meal. He prepared his bed near the fire where it would be in the shadows. As he sat by the flames, he kept a path open into the shadows where he could move back if the need arose.

Tonight, that need came. As he sat drinking his coffee, Goliath turned his ears toward the darkness upstream. Jedidah could see his nostrils flaring as the horse sensed something in the dark. "Hello in the camp. I mean no harm, but I smelled your coffee, and I haven't had any in days."

"Who are you and what do you want?" Jediah asked.

"Just a lone rider looking for a cup of coffee and perhaps some food."

Jedidiah told him to come in slowly and keep his hands away from his iron. The stranger walked into his camp leading his horse by the reins. The stranger said thank you as he tied his horse. They sat across from each other sipping their coffee and sizing each other up. Finally, the stranger asked who and what he was doing out there alone. Jedidiah told him he was trailing three men who had killed a friend and his sister. He then told him that there had been four, but he had already killed one.

"The name's Jedidiah. What's yours?"

Holding the cup of coffee in both hands and looking Jedidiah straight in the eye, he told him his name. "William Bonney."

Jedidiah said, "Seems I have heard of you."

"They call me Billy the Kid. I've heard of you, too," William said. "I heard that Buffalo Bill said a small man shot a bandit in Emporia and the little gun was as fast as he had seen."

"I heard you are pretty fast, too," Jedidiah stated. "Hope I never have to find out for sure. The only ones I'm after are the men who killed my sister."

"That's good enough for me," Billy the Kid said. "I am moving on to New Mexico territory myself. I hope to find distraction in Elizabeth Town."

"I figured I'd go to Dodge City but stop off in Hutchinson first." Said Jedidiah.

"Mind if I ride along for a while?" asked Billy.

Jedidiah told him he could do as he pleased but that he normally didn't get along with others well, except for an old trapper that the four men killed. Billy the Kid told him he didn't have anything against him, and they could rest easier by riding together. Billy then told Jedidiah he could ride with him to this side of Dodge, but that he wasn't going into that town. He planned on turning southwest before going on to Elizabeth Town.

The next day they rode into a low, dry creek bed. They rested their horses and practiced fast draw and shooting. They exchanged a few techniques and gave each other some tips. They had already discovered that they were nearly the same age and were becoming friends. As they rode, Jedidiah learned that riding with another made the day go faster and easier. He soon learned to trust his new friend, to watch his side of the trail, which eased the load and strain of keeping a close eye. Billy was also some help in setting up camp at night.

One morning after breaking camp, they rode quietly, each searching the horizon slowly. Both of their horses' ears perked up and they looked to the right. Jedidiah looked at Billy the Kid who in turn looked at him. Something was off to their right.

Billy the Kid rode to Jedidiah's right side. Jedidiah continued watching left but occasionally looked off to the right. A short time later, Billy whispered, "There's an Indian riding just over the hill pacing us. There hadn't been any trouble lately, but you can never tell what an Indian might be after. Might just be a young buck looking to take some trophies." They continued watching and an hour later, Billy whispered, "He's back."

Jedidiah slowly looked to the right to see a lone Indian riding along the ridge north of them. The Indian had shadowed them for most of the day.

Just before dark, they spotted a mesa six feet uphill from a running creek. There was a tree with high branches which would be a good place for a campfire. They each cared for their horses before starting a cook fire. Jedidiah was just moving to pour a cup of coffee when he looked up to see the Indian standing before them. Jedidiah poured the coffee and offered it to the Indian.

Taking the coffee, the Indian pointed to his chest and said, in English, "Piachiti I am Kickapoo." He was traveling to his tribe. Piachiti had been with the tribe of his bride for a year. Billy offered him some food, and they sat and talked while they ate. Piachiti told them that he had worked with his bride's family for a year as was their custom. Though some no longer adhered to the old customs, his family and those of his bride did. He was to return to his home and prepare a lodge for him and his bride. They would follow in four moons then he and his bride would be united.

Jedidiah told Piachiti he was traveling to Dodge and that William was going southwest into the New Mexico territory. "We are traveling together for a few more days."

Piachiti said he would travel with them for two days before he would turn north toward his tribe's land. He told them that they were raising corn and wheat. They carried water from a creek for now. He had been to a school and would now help the tribe to build a reservoir and irrigation ditches. Jedidiah told him that it sounded like a good idea and should help the tribe.

Piachiti asked Jedidiah about his quest. "Are you looking for gold and your fortune in the west?"

Jedidiah explained about the men he was chasing. Billy asked Piachiti why he had followed them. Piachiti told them he was mystified at the small man riding the giant horse. He watched them set up their camp and decided to just walk in and learn about them. Piachiti then told Jedidiah that for such a small man he had a large way about him.

" What about me?" Billy the Kid asked.

Piachiti looked at him and said, "You have the way of death walking with you on this trail of life". The usual smile left Billy's face, and he looked down kicking at the ground. It was as if the Kickapoo Indian had foretold his destiny.

They all woke up before dawn and were riding at first light. They rode mostly in silence all day watching for possible trouble. Jedidiah was constantly watching for signs of the men he chased.

That night in camp, Billy seemed even more gloomy. Jedidiah and Piachiti talked till the fire had faded down. The Kickapoo believed the little man to be very brave–so small and young going out against four killers. Piachiti said he would have done no less, but to see it in such a little white little man was uncommon. The next morning, they rode together. When the sun was high in the sky, Piachiti told them he was turning north here, adding that they would be coming into a white man settlement by midday tomorrow. He had no desire to go there. They all wished each other well and rode on.

That night, Jedidiah asked Billy what was bothering him.

"I've been told before I was on a path of death. I didn't want to believe it. I started out seeking justice but then it turned to vengeance. Now I feel nothing when I take a man's life."

The next afternoon they rode together into Hutchison. The few people on the street looked at them though nobody said a thing. There were a few that whispered. "Billy the Kid."

Billy looked at Jedidiah and told him he would probably be going south and then west from here. Since Jedidiah would be going northwest, they would be parting ways once they left Hutchison. Jedidiah told him he was going to the sheriff's office to find out if they knew anything about the men he was chasing.

Mathew looked at the little man strolling into the sheriff's office and he recognized the lone cowboy right away from the telegram he received from Emporia. "Come on in and have a seat, Jedidiah."

"You know who I am," Jedidiah stated.

"From the telegram," Mathew said. "And those outlaws have already been through here. Two days ago. A rider came in saying the railroad payroll had been jobbed. The three rode out in a hurry, and I sent a posse after them. But they lost them that afternoon in a sandstorm. No tracks left and no way to tell which way they rode from there. I have their names, though, if that would help." Jedidiah nodded. "Jake Allister, his brother, George Allister, and Cousin Lester Brest."

Jedidiah thanked him and said, "I'm sure they're moving on to Dodge. I heard something about cutting some herds."

"There's bad news in the area, then, if they intended to steal cattle from the cattle drives coming up from Texas," Mathew said. "The trains are coming this way to haul the cattle back east. The buyers are moving in to meet the drives. Nobody wants to see that disrupted, but some of the outlaw's plan to do just that by cutting the herds. I'll send word to Wyatt Earp in Dodge."

Jedidiah told Mathew he would be riding out as soon as he sent a wire and bought some supplies. Stopping at the telegraph office he sent a message to the sheriff back home, informing him of his location and that his next stop would be Dodge. Jedidiah then went to the general store and bought some beans, coffee, salt, and other supplies. He packed everything up and climbed on Goliath. Billy rode out to the west end of town with him before turning south. "I need to move on before the sheriff finds a paper on me." They wished each other luck and said their goodbyes.

Jedidiah turned Goliath west alongside the railroad bed. After following the tracks for a short distance, he angled away for a mile. Away from the railroad he scouted for a creek or river to spend the night by. Alone again, he figured he would travel faster and try to catch up with the three outlaws. *If I really push it, I can be in Dodge in four days, Jedidiah thought.* He would have to stop late and move out before dawn each morning.

The first night he made camp two hours after the sun had set. Once he had rubbed Goliath down, he fixed a quick meal. He slept in the shadows as the last ember of his fire faded away. In the morning, he rode again, staying a mile or so from the workers building the railroad. Along the way he decided to ride into one of the workers' camps as he passed. Perhaps they might know something of the Allister brothers' gang. That was what Mathew called them. Mathew also said he would let the railroad people know he was tracking the outlaws and asked for their help.

In the first camp he rode into, no one saw or heard anything. The next afternoon he rode into a camp that had seen the brothers. Jake, Lester, and George had stopped there, and the workers had been prepared for them. As the brothers rode into camp, they were met with a dozen men with rifles in hand. They hustled out of camp on the run. Jedidiah was only a few hours behind them. After saying, "thank you to them," he pushed on towards Dodge.

Chapter 5: Dodge

Jake, George, and Lester stopped along a winding river two miles from the railroad. They had dusted their trail, riding hard to get away from all those guns. Jake told them they would put the railroad on hold for now. They would cut south of Dodge and try to pick up the trail of a herd going north. Once they found a herd, they would slip in and cut out a few heads each night. Till they caught up with a herd, they would look for a box canyon where they could pen the cattle until they were ready to sell them. "Once we have skimmed off the cream of the cattle business, we will go west to the gold field," Jake said.

The three rode together for two more days and found the perfect canyon. The north end of the canyon was closed, with a spring-fed creek and a narrow passage which they could fence off. There was plenty of green grass around the flowing creek. Fifty to a hundred head of cattle could be held here for a few days. Jake, George, and Lester hurriedly built a fence that they could close once the cattle were pushed into the canyon. They rode out from there, watching for a herd. On every high hilltop, they scanned the horizon looking for dust clouds. Large herds of cattle on a trail made a mighty dust cloud that could be seen for miles.

In the afternoon they looked around to see such a cloud, and it was moving north. They rode along the east side of the herd staying out of sight. Once the herd stopped for the night, they watched and waited for their chance. The cowboys were changing shifts watching the herd every two hours. Three thirty in the morning they moved to the rear of the herd and silently separated two dozen of the cattle, moving them to the canyon they had prepared a holding pen in. They would rest till late afternoon and easily catch the herd before it bedded down for the night again.

Loyd, one of the night riders, rode along the right flank of the herd. Some movement to his right along a hill caught his eye. He stopped his horse near a tree looking toward the hill. Three men drove a dozen head of cattle over a ridge to the northeast. Loyd realized that they were cutting the herd. He rode to camp and nudged the boss to wake him up. "Boss, some men are cutting cattle from the rear of the herd and driving them east. The boss woke up the camp and had one of the hands ride ahead to Dodge to tell the marshal. The next night he was sure that they had more cattle cut out from the herd. He was ready to send all his men out hunting the cutters. Wyatt Earp and three others, dressed in black dusters and hats and carrying six-shooters, rode into camp. Wyatt told him he had an idea who was cutting his herd, and he would go after them. That night, the Allister gang once again moved in from the rear on to the bedded-down herd. They cut out a few more heads and pushed them to the canyon. This would probably be the last time they hit this herd as the herd would move close to Dodge the next day. As the first glow of dawn peaked out, they moved the cattle into the canyon and closed the fence.

Jake felt, as much as he heard, something behind him. He turned to see men riding toward them fast. Jake gave no thought to anything but getting away. He kicked spurs to his horse and pointed his head south. George, being closely attuned to his brother, didn't ask questions but lit a shuck too. Lester turned to see what was happening and came face to face with three rifles pointed at him. He knew he didn't have a chance but hoped that his cousins would bust him out.

Wyat and his men took Lester to Dodge, stopping to tell the cattle drive where their missing cattle were. They also informed the trail boss that the Arkansas River in Dodge was dry and that the railroad hadn't arrived there yet. They were expecting them soon though. Wyatt told them of a spring fed creek with good grazing sixteen miles south of Dodge that would be a good place for them to hold the cattle awhile.

Lester was placed in the Dodge jail to await trial. Wyatt had determined they were the men wanted for the railroad robbery and the murder back in Missouri. He also received a wire saying that Jedidiah was on his way there. If he got there in time, he could testify about the murder at Lester's trial, and they would hang him. If not, he would be going to prison with hard labor for at least ten years.

Jedidiah had ridden a lonesome hard trail since leaving Hutchison. Twice he rode into railroad camps asking about the men. Each time, he heard the same thing, with no sign of the men. He had no idea what they were up to now. Jedidiah pushed on towards Dodge. He stopped and made a dry camp two miles north of the old Fort Dodge and about four miles east of Dodge. His camp was near the railroad, and he had noticed that the construction was coming right along. Here, they were almost ready for the steel rails, which would come with the first trains. He had seen them as they laid track back up the line, the engine would be pushing the flat cars with the rails on it. Dozens of men worked laying the track and nailing it down. They were not moving as fast as he had been, but they could be showing up in Dodge within another week or two.

The next morning, Jedidiah saddled Goliath before dawn. As the sun came up, he rode into Dodge with the sunrise behind him. Wyatt was just walking out of the Dodge House from eating his breakfast when he saw a silhouette of someone coming into town. Wyatt removed the strap off his six-gun. Once he saw the little man on the big Morgan horse, he smiled and said, "Good morning, Jedidiah."

The two walked together to the jail as Wyatt told Jedidiah about capturing Lester. Wyatt looked closely at the short gunman's face. One eyebrow was raised but he had a determined look about him. "Are you ready to face up to one of the men you have been chasing for so long," asked Wyatt? Jedidiah just nodded his head up and down thinking, *what would this man that killed my sister be like*? The sheriff took Jedidiah's gun before allowing him back into the cell block. Wyatt opened the door to the block and closed it behind Jedidiah.

Walking into the cell block he could see two cells on either side of the narrow aisle. Lester was in the second cell on the right side. Jedidiah asked Lester if he remembered his sister back in Missouri and what they had done to her. Lester wasn't a coward, but he felt fear then, for he knew that instead of spending time in jail he might hang.

Jedidiah told Wyatt that Lester was one of the men who killed his sister and the old trapper he had worked for. The sheriff asked Jedidiah if he would stay for the trial and testify it should be in the next two days? Jedidiah told him he would and that he would be there till the killer was hung. After that he would move on to look for the other two. The sheriff told him he would send out wires asking for any information about the whereabouts of the others. Jedidiah went from the sheriff's office to the telegraph office. There was a wire for him from Missouri along with a bank draft for some money. The telegraph stated that the sheriff there thought he might be running low on cash and sent him some of his rent money. Jedidiah sent a wire back to the sheriff telling him that Lester was in jail pending a trial.

From the telegraph office Jedidiah went to the Dodge House to eat and see about a room. He intended to stay there till the hanging. He then took Goliath to the livery stable telling the owner to take good care of him. He paid the owner well knowing he would care for his one true friend Goliath. After he went to his room to clean up and get some rest. He had been riding hard for days and was worn out.

Jedidiah woke up in the evening to loud music and whooping and hollering. He checked his gun before strapping it on and went to eat. One of the deputies came to him at the cafe and told him the trial would be tomorrow at nine o'clock. Jedidiah told the deputy he would be there ready to testify. He then finished his meal and went back to the boarding house and his room.

In the morning Jedidiah had breakfast in the dining room, which was full. Many people came overnight for the trial. Nobody paid much attention to him as he ate. The talk was all about the trial. They said that Lester had been a part of a group that had robbed the railroad payroll and tried cutting the cattle herd coming in soon. There was a railroad worker here along with some men from the cattle drive; all were present to testify against the defendant. Then the talk turned to one man saying he had heard that there was a witness who would testify that the outlaws murdered someone in Missouri and that would be added to the charges. If so, Lester would surely be hanged, and it would certainly happen within the next two days.

Jedidiah walked to the livery stable to see Goliath. He gave the massive horse a cube of sugar and talked to him. From the stable he went to the sheriff's office and talked to Wyat about the trial. Jedidiah was curious about what to expect as he had never been to a trial before. He then went to the saloon where the trial was to be held. People were beginning to gather, and a deputy was standing at the door. A table with a chair was on one side of the room to the right of the bar. The other chairs were placed facing that table. A dozen seats were placed against the wall by the street for the jurors. The deputy took Jedidiah to a seat near the front where he sat down to wait.

A few minutes later, Wyatt and two more deputies brought the prisoner in and sat him down on the front row to the right of the table. Two drovers and two railroad workers were escorted in and seated by Jedidiah. Then the room filled up with all others that wished to observe. Once the room was filled, Wyatt asked, "Everyone stand and put out your smokes." He also announced, "the bar was closed." The judge walked in and sat behind the table. Wyatt then told the people they could sit down.

As Lester was led into the courtroom, he held out hope that he might get away or be released. At worst he thought he might spend a few years in prison. His cousins might even break him out of prison.

The judge pounded his gavel and asked the prosecutor, "What are the charges against the defendant?"

The prosecutor said, "Two counts of robbing the railroad, one count of cattle theft, one count of rape, and two counts of murder."

When the prosecutor stated the charges and included rape and murder, Lester feared he might hang.

The judge looked at the defendant and asked, "How do you plead?"

Lester knew if he admitted to the charges, he would hang, so he said, "I'm innocent."

The first witness who was called was a railroad worker. He testified that he saw the defendant and two others rob the supply wagon with the payroll. The second witness also testified to seeing them rob a different supply wagon. The next witness was a drover that was on night shift. He had seen them taking cattle from the herd. He testified he spotted them as they went over a ridge and skylighted themselves. The other drover testified that Lester and his men had stolen cattle the next night. Wyatt then testified that he had caught them with the stolen cattle.

The prosecutor then called Jedidiah to the stand. Jedidiah was asked who he was and why he had come to Kansas.

He told them about the trapper and how he had been robbed and killed. He then talked about how the four men came into town and spent a lot of money. The sheriff there had later told him that his sister had been raped and killed that night. The sheriff gave him some of the money they had spent, and it was earmarked just like the trapper would split the money that he was to give to Jedidiah. He pulled that money out of his pocket and showed it to the judge. He then went into detail of how his sister had been found and what all they had done to her.

" My sister was all I had," Jedidiah stated. "Our parents died years before." As he talked, Lester hung his head, knowing he would soon hang. The prosecutor asked Jedidah about the fourth man. He told them he caught up with them in Emporia and tried to take Brody to the sheriff. However, Brody reached for his gun, and Jedidiah had outdrawn him. " I shot him in the head and Buffalo Bill Cody witnessed it."

Jedidiah then explained to the judge that Cody told the sheriff how it happened and that it was a fair fight. A few of the men in the courtroom looked at Jedidiah with a little more respect.

The jury only took ten minutes to deliberate. They came in and each one in turn said, "Guilty."

The judge told the prisoner to stand and then told him that at noon the next day he would be hung by the neck till dead. Jedidiah nodded his head in agreement, with a slight smile on his face. Wyatt and the deputies took Lester back to the jail and took turns watching over him.

After the trial, Jedidiah went to buy supplies as he planned on leaving Dodge right after the hanging. He then went to check if he had any telegraphs, which he was expecting but still had not come. Though he didn't like associating in a saloon, that was his next stop. It was often the best location to learn about the trails ahead. Half of the drovers were in the saloon at this time. Jedidah got a beer and sat to listen to the talk. Once the talk about the trial faded, the discussion went to the trails around the area. Jedidiah perked his ears to listen. One thing he quickly learned was that good water was difficult to find. The drover spoke of a place far to the south called Norice that had good water. One of the surveyors for the railroad said that he knew of the place, and they were looking to go that way once the tracks were in full operation to Dodge. He also added that they were looking to go southwest. There was a man out there with good water, and he was liberal with it. The talk then went to what they were going to do once the herd was sold. One of the men said he was tired of punching cattle and had a hankering to go to Elizebeth town. He had heard there was a gold boom there. He wanted to try his hand at panning for gold. He said he could always return to Texas if he didn't have any luck. One of the other men said he thought he would join him if he didn't mind.

Jedidiah had pretty much gone unnoticed by the drovers till a railroad worker said, "Little man, did you really outdraw that outlaw in Emporia and right in front of Bill Cody?"

"I did," Jedidiah responded, "and it had been seventy yards. I hit him right between the eyes. His gun went off into the ground not five feet in front of him. Bill said it was as fast a draw as he had ever seen. I met another guy that was faster than me though. William Bonney. He helped me some, along the trail."

One of the men asked, "Did you meet Billy the Kid?'

Jedidiah told them, "Yep. We shared the trail for a few days. One afternoon, we did a little target practice. One of the cowboys told him he was one lucky fellow, that Billy the Kid had killed several men. I found William friendly and helpful.

A railroad worker declared, "For a little man, you have some big friends! Billy the Kid and Buffalo Bill Cody!"

Jedidiah said, "Now I count Wyatt Earp as a friend also." He finished his beer and walked out of the saloon with everyone inside watching him as he left. Jedidiah thought he might hear laughter as he went out the door, but he heard none.

Before heading to dinner, Jedidiah went to the sheriff's office. Wyatt walked with him. "I captured Lester and sent off for the reward," Wyat said, "but rightfully it should be yours. Your friends and townsfolk back in Missouri put up that reward and you've been tracking him all the way here. You are going to need it if you are going after the two brothers." Then Wyatt told him, "I heard the brothers are going toward the New Mexico territory. There isn't much south or west of here and little water."

At the sheriff's office, Jedidiah was told about a man called Roundtree in town with the herd and that he might wish to talk with him. Roundtree had ridden over much of that area and gave him some good advice about travelling through it. Jedidiah thanked Wyatt and the sheriff and left the office.

Back at the saloon, Jedidiah asked for Roundtree. One of the drovers stood up and said, "I'm Roundtree." He hadn't said anything while Jedidiah had been there before. He was an older man wearing buckskin and carrying his gun low.

Wyatt said, "I might get some advice about the trails. There's a steak dinner in it for you if you care to join me."

"Well, I'd be downright pleased, young man," Roundtree said.

They walked out together to the Dodge house and ordered steaks with the fixings. Roundtree asked what he wanted to know.

"Everything I should know to cross the area and find the men I'm after," Jedidiah said.

Though not much of a talker, Roundtree opened up describing the flat lands and what was there. He explained where he could find water when it seemed there was none to be found. He told him that he might ride for days without seeing a tree, but he could use buffalo chips for fire.

Roundtree then told him that there were some mighty dangerous Indians out there. The Comanche, Kiowa, and the Apache. Any of them would lift a man's hair. Roundtree then told him about the weather. "The wind blows most of the time. It can blow so hard as to make a man ride on the side of his horse to the downwind. Then all of a sudden, a mighty storm can blow in with a twister blowing everything away. It might pour down rain for an hour then be dry and blowing sand an hour after that. Best when that happens to find a gully and lay flat till it's past. Cover your horse's head and your own with a blanket till the wind blows out. Them Apache… you most likely will never see one. If you do, he will probably already have you and test your worth. They take stock in how strong a man they catch. They will torture you till you're finished. The longer a man lasts, the stronger he is, and the greater the mettle they get from him. Out there high up on the mesa there is a fortress. It is not a safe place; it is an outlaw hang out. Sometimes up to thirty mean outlaws are there. It is a mighty fortress, too, with thick stone walls and no windows, just slits to shoot out of. It can be a rough place to cross but once you're to the other side, there are the highest mountains you'll ever see. They rise straight up into the clouds. They call them the Rockies nowadays. It is a beautiful place if you make it that far."

After talking to Roundtree, Jedidiah went to his room. He got up early the next morning for breakfast in the boarding house. Wyatt came in and told him he had heard the two brothers were south and west going into the badlands. He figured that they were headed to the outlaw fortress. Jedidiah told the sheriff that he would be riding out as soon as the hanging was over. He had everything he needed and would be saddled and ready by noon.

In Dodge, when it came to a hanging, a lift at the livery stable was used. It was a beam from the loft used to lift loads to a door in the loft. It extended three feet from the door in front of the stable. As the deputies led Lester out to the livery stable, Wyatt looked around to see Jedidiah sitting astride Goliath. He was packed and ready to ride. They put Lester on the back of a large freight wagon with a team and a deputy on the reins. They placed the hangman's noose around Lester's neck and Wyatt nodded his head to the deputy. The deputy then popped his whip over the team, and they bolted off. Lester dropped off the back of the wagon and hung from the lift. Lester kicked twice then it was over.

Jedidiah watched, then nodded goodbye to Wyatte before riding away.

Chapter 6: The Badlands

Jake and George had ridden away from the ambush leaving Lester behind. They rode for two days going south near the border of Oklahoma territory. They camped along a creek. Water was few and far between. George built a fire, and while sitting around it, they heard from the darkness, "Hello in the camp." Both reached for their guns and heard the voice say, "If I was going to kill you, I could have done it already."

Jake asked, "Who are you and what do you want?"

"Just a stranger traveling west looking for a cup of coffee."

"Come on in, easy like," Jake said. He and George both had their rifles in hand but pointed them down.

The young man riding a roan came into the camp with his hand near his gun. He told them, "Put the rifles down before I drop you both."

"Who do you think you are? Jake asked.

"The name's William Bonney."

Jake and George both dropped their rifles like they were on fire. Jake asked Billy the Kid where he was going and was told the New Mexico territory. Billy told them he was looking for a less crowded place. George told Billy they were looking for opportunities.

” You should go to the Fortress. They might use some more guns,” Bill the Kid said. Jake asked him about it and what they were doing. “I heard they were hitting wagon trains going west on the Santa Fe trail, killing and taking what they could find.” Jake asked him if he was going to hook up with them. Billy told him no. “It seems too petty for me and too small a take. I’m going where trouble is and they need a gun. I am about as good as they come with a gun.”

Jake asked, “What can we expect at the Fortress?”

“If you’re sure you want to go there, you should ride slowly up to the entrance. Make certain that your hands are nowhere near your weapons. Stop well before the door and wait for a challenge. Once they ask who you are and what you want, tell them and leave nothing out. If they turn you back, ask for some water. You will need it, as there isn’t any other water for miles. They may or may not give you some, but do not try to push your way in. There will be many guns pointed at you.”

Jake asked Billy if he was going the same way, to which he responded, “I’m taking a different trail in the morning… passing onto a trail further south.”

The next morning, Billy the Kid went south then west. A day later he was at a small shack by a running river. It was a line shack with two cowboys staying there. After a cup of coffee, he told them about the brothers and that they were wanted by a friend of his. He asked them if they could send word to Dodge for Jedidiah that the men he was after were going to the Fortress.

...

The morning of Lester's hanging, Wyatt had a telegraph from a cowhand telling him the men Jedidiah was hunting were going to the Fortress. He showed the telegraph to Jedidiah and to Roundtree. Jedidiah was advised if he went to the Fortress to keep his hands free of weapons and to stop in front of the entrance and wait. "Tell them who it is you're looking for and what they did to your sister. They probably won't let you in, but if the brothers are in there, they may kick them out after you leave. Most outlaws will not abide with someone who molests a girl. There are too few of them out here, especially pretty ones."

After the hanging, Wyatt looked back to Jedidiah and nodded to him. Jedidiah turned Goliath toward the edge of Dodge and rode out of town. Tied to his saddle was six large canteens of water along with grub to last four weeks. The grub was mostly salt, coffee, flour, dried beans and some canned meat. Most of the meat he would hunt along the way. He would also fish and gather some greens, fruits, and berries on the trail. Once he left Dodge, Jedidiah did not see much but a flat open prairie. As the sun was setting, he had not found a creek or anyplace that might serve as a campsite. A pheasant flew up in front of him, and he shot it and cleaned it while riding on. Right at dark, he came to a low gully that looked like a dry creek bed. He decided to camp there. He rubbed Goliath down and gave him some water. He staked him out to graze for the evening. He then built a small fire and cooked the pheasant.

The next morning, he made a small fire to brew coffee then saddled Goliath and moved out. He finished off the pheasant along with a piece of bread. Jedidiah rode south by west all day without seeing much. Occasionally, there would be a ravine but with no water. Jedidiah did not push the trail as it was long and dry. The only water so far were the six canteens carried on Goliath's back. On the third night, two hours before sunset, he found a clear flowing creek with a few trees. Jedidiah crossed the creek and looked for a good campsite. He and Goliath drank their fill and replenished all the canteens with fresh water. He caught three fish out of the creek and cooked them. The next morning, he caught another fish and enjoyed it with coffee. He watered Goliath and drank his fill before saddling up.

He camped along a dry gulch the next night. Not long after riding away from the camp, he saw a half dozen Indians riding into view from the north. They came up close enough to get a good look at him then turned and ran away back to the north. He had his hand on his gun but didn't think that was why they ran. They looked like they had seen a ghost the way they lit out. They must have never seen a man under four-foot-tall sitting on top of a giant horse.

Just before noon the next day, Jedidiah saw a few trees and a small building. A man rode up to the building from the side with a hoe in his hand. "Well, I'll be darn," he said. "You're the smallest man I've ever seen and that's the biggest horse I've ever seen. You might as well get on down and have some water. I'm sure you're dry by now."

As Jedidiah was getting down off Goliath, he said, "We certainly are, sir, and I thank you."

The man introduced himself as Seymour Rodgers and offered Jedidiah a meal or two. He then told him he had plenty of food but was out of coffee. Jedidiah told him he had plenty of coffee and would be happy to share some with him. Goliath was able to graze on fresh green grass and have his fill of water. Jedidiah helped Seymour in his garden that afternoon then sat in the shade to drink cool water. They had fresh buffalo steaks that night and vegetables from the garden.

Seymour told Jedidiah that if he was going to the Fortress, to go due west till he came to the Cimarron River. "Follow it to Robbers Roost," Seymour added. 'The fortress is atop it. The river comes out from behind some mesas on the south side of the Roost. The Cimarron is a four-day ride so go easy on drinking, to conserve water. You'll be hard pressed to find any on that trail. There are a few creeks to cross, but they are most likely to be dry. The Cimarron, even if not running, will have regular water holes."

Jedidiah left some of his coffee with Seymour. He had filled all his canteens. At dawn the next morning he rode out straight west. A little before sunset he happened upon a buffalo wallow. It was about half full of muddy water. Goliath wasn't finicky and drank his fill. Jedidiah decided to camp there for the night. There wasn't a piece of wood in sight, so he gathered some chips for a small fire. He piled enough chips to the side for a morning fire. He cared for Goliath and made some coffee. The fire had burnt down by sunset, and he stretched out to sleep.

Jedidiah woke before dawn and started the fire to make some coffee. While it was brewing, he gathered his belongings and saddled Goliath. As the sun came up, he rode with his back to the rising dawn. He rode slow and easy, not pushing Goliath. From what Seymour had told him; he would be lucky to find more water for another three days. The water in his canteens would last that long if he was careful with it. He had dry goods in his supplies to last if he supplemented it with some game. Out here though, the game seemed to be as scarce as the water. He rode slowly till the sun was low on the horizon. He saw a pheasant and was able to shoot it. He made camp his second night out from Seymour's place and cooked the pheasant. As he ate the pheasant, he thought to himself, *one more night and by the next, I should be on the river.* He let Goliath drink half of the canteen he was using before he made his coffee.

Again, he rode out right at sunrise. The coolest and best riding was early morning. The air was fresh and every day there was some wind. Today, however, there was none; it was calm and extremely quiet all day. The heat hung in the air like a thick blanket. Even the air itself seemed to weigh him down. All day, he felt like something was wrong. Jedidiah stayed alert, gazing right to left, throughout the day, riding slow and listening. Sometimes when he rode, he sang or whistled, but not today. As dusk came, the western horizon became reddish brown. He knew the weather was coming. He picketed Goliath close to him that night and went to bed early.

Before dawn the next morning, Jedidiah was back on the trail, riding harder than they had on this leg of his journey. It would be the day he reached Cimarron. By noon, the wind was blowing strong from the south. By mid-afternoon, it was so hard that it was difficult for him to stay in the saddle. Two hours later, he was sure he could see a line of broken trees on the horizon. It was a good sign of

the river. The closer he came to it, the more he was sure
that was the river he was looking for. By this time, a dark
line of clouds had risen over the western horizon.

A storm was coming. He thought of the advice that
old Rountree gave him. He pushed onto the river and
looked for a good place to camp. Since he was going to
follow the river, it didn't matter which side he camped on.
He wanted some shelter below the flats but well above the
water line. Jedidiah found a bench on the west side of the
river. It was bracketed with tall oak trees and five feet
below the flat land. It was eight feet above the water which
should keep him and Goliath out of the river. He worked
quickly to build a shelter to keep him and his gear dry. As
soon as he had finished that, he staked Goliath out and
rubbed him down. He built a fire and then the rain came.
Ice fell from the sky the size of his fist. Then it poured rain.
Just to the south, he could hear a loud roar, and the wind
blew like he had never seen before. Minutes later it was all
over, and the stars were shining. The wind blew hard from
the west which he was protected by the hill in that
direction.

The next morning was cooler, and the wind blew
from the north. He rested till late in the morning, caring for
Goliath. He killed a couple of rabbits and cooked them. It
was mid-morning before he rode south along the river. It
was running today, and he hoped that it would continue to.
According to what Seymour had told him, it should only be
two days' ride to the Fortress. He wanted to come around
that bend at dawn and ride out of the rising sun. Jedidiah
hoped that it would give him the edge. Would he finally

catch up with the last two men or would they elude him again, he wondered.

At times, he was able to cut off a few miles by seeing a straight path to a bend in the river. The Cimarron, like most rivers, wound around like a snake with many bends and curves. Late in the afternoon in the far distance, he could see the mesa rising up before him. Much closer was a bend in the river that, from a distance, looked to provide a good campsite. He camped there with a small fire right at sunset, drinking his coffee and thinking about tomorrow. He would be close to the Fortress. He had no notion that he could take on twenty to thirty outlaws, much less some inside a fortress. All he knew for certain was that he was hunting the last two men who killed his sister.

In the middle of the afternoon the next day he was riding slow and easy. Jedidiah was sure that he was close. The river was going west at the time with high hills rising on either side. Just up ahead, he saw the river turned more northerly, and he eased up to the bend. He rode Goliath closer to the hillside on his right as he came to the bend. The river went a short distance and turned back west. A great hill curved with the river about five hundred yards to the north. He rode along the edge of that hill. As he came to the point of the hill, he could see a valley with a creek coming from the north to drain into the Cimarron. Right on the east side of that creek was an escarpment. A single mount rising from the valley. From where he sat on Goliath, he could see a trail winding up and around the east side. He had no doubt that the Fortress lay at the top. He turned around and rode back to the east around the bend.

A dry creek bed came down from the mountains east of the Robbers Roost. Jedidiah rode back to the creek bed and then north through a pass between those hills. He found a peak near the east side of the Roost and rode up close to the peak. He tied Goliath to some scrub brush and climbed to the top. From here he could see the east side to Robbers Roost. Just below the peak on the northeast side was the Fortress. If they were watching, there would be no way to ride up there without being seen.

While he was riding up, he noticed a place on the other side of the trail that might be a spring or a tank. Now Roundtree had told him about the tanks in these hills. They were rocky depressions that held water after a rain. He went back there to camp for the night. He made a dry camp and rubbed Goliath down good. They had found the tank and had plenty of water. He remained quiet all night. Most of the time he thought about the men and what they had done to his sister. Then he thought about her. He could barely remember what she looked like anymore. He thought of the old trapper and how he had befriended him. Tomorrow, he would find out if the brothers were here.

Chapter 7: Robbers Roost

Jedidiah was awake long before dawn. He ate a little jerky and drank water. He then rubbed Goliath down, watered him and fed him some grain. He rode to the bend and was sitting on Goliath there as the sun came up behind him. He went straight to the trail up Robbers Roost. Jedidiah stopped Goliath a hundred yards before the entrance. The building was hand laid with heavy stone. The back looked to be right up against a huge drop to the valley floor below on the north side. There were no windows, just several slits in the stone barely large enough for a shooter to fire from. The only door he could see was a massive wood door facing him.

He heard a woman's voice state, "Who are you and what do you want?"

"I'm Jedidiah, and I'm looking for two men who raped and killed my sister. Their names are Jake and George Allister. I don't want any trouble or anybody else, just those two."

The woman said, "They are not here. The men all left to go to Las Vegas." Just then Jedidiah heard a boom and felt a hard slap to his left side. He looked down to see blood coming from his left lower abdomen. He felt faint just as Goliath bolted with him turning and running down the hill. Jedidiah grabbed a hold of the pommel as Goliath ran to the river and turned west. Jedidiah stayed in the saddle somehow as Goliath ran west along the river. Jedidiah didn't know how long or how far they ran, but Goliath finally stopped running and was drinking in the river.

After Jedidiah had passed out, he came to, still in the saddle. He knew he had been shot and needed to care for the wound. He also knew that there was nobody to do it for him. If he was to live, he would have to care for himself. He managed to climb out of the saddle and remove it from Goliath. He then hobbled him so that he wouldn't go far. He managed to build a fire and started some coffee brewing. He then placed some jerky in a pot of water to boil. This would make some broth which would help him get his strength back. He then looked at his wound. Feeling both sides he could tell the bullet had passed clean through. It just caught him on the far-left side of his belly. He was sure that it hadn't damaged anything vital, but it hurt like hell. He washed it the best he could and smeared tree moss that he found near the river on both wounds. He wasn't sure if that was the right thing or not but remembered the trapper saying something about using tree moss before. He drank coffee and most of the broth before he passed out.

Jedidiah woke up at daybreak feeling the warmth from the fire. As his eyes came more into focus, he could see several Indians squatted around watching him. He looked down to see that they had put some kind of poultice on his wounds. As his eyes moved back up, he could see his rifle and handgun laying not far to his right side. He looked right at the nearest Indian who seemed to be in charge. He didn't think they meant any harm or else they wouldn't have helped him. Jedidiah told them he didn't speak Indian. The Indian in front of him told him he spoke to a little white man's tongue. A woman came to him with some broth which he drank. Then he passed out again.

Sometime later he woke up to see his guns still nearby. A woman got up and gave him some more broth and a little meat. Jedidiah wasn't sure what the meat was, but he ate it. The woman walked away, and the male Indian came back. They talked some and the Indian wanted to know why he had attacked the white man fortress. He told him about the men he was after. Jedidiah told him his name, and he learned that the Indian's name was Tosahwi or White Knife and that he was the son of Buffalo Hump, Comanche Chief. He was told they were going home to Indian territory from taking his father to a burial ground in the mountain that smoked. It was a mountain that smoked many years ago but does not anymore. It was their old burial ground and where his father wanted to go. Tosahwi then told him they had watched him go up to the fortress and followed him there. They thought he was brave and had strong spirits. Jedidiah thanked him for helping him. They asked if he was coming here to hunt buffalo. Jedidiah told them he was hunting bad men. Then he told them about the men he chased and what they had done. Tosahwi told him they would stay two more days and help him heal, then they would travel on to their home.

Jedidiah gained strength quickly and learned a few words of Comanche. He was amazed that they helped him rather than killed him. Jedidiah learned that Tosahwi had been taught English at a mission school near the place they now lived. Watching them as they worked around the camp, Jedidiah gained respect for his new Indian friends. A few would ride out in the mornings to hunt. At all times one or more would be watching from a hidden location. Then one morning, he woke up to look around, and they were all gone. They had left sometime during the night or just before dawn. His guns were still right where they had been left. He had never touched them till now. He picked up his six gun and checked the cylinder. It was full. He cleaned it and strapped it on. He then checked his rifle, and it too was fully loaded.

Jedidiah fixed breakfast and some coffee. He walked about for a spell looking the area over well. The Comanche had left a hind quarter of an antelope hanging in the camp for him. He appreciated all they had done. He also resolved himself to pass on the sentiment to others that might be in need. After walking around a bit, he knew he wasn't ready to ride yet, but maybe tomorrow. The Comanche had told him what to expect between here and Las Vegas. They told him that this river was the dry Cimmaron. Four or five days ride southwest of here was the Cimmaron in a deep canyon. It flowed from the mountains past Rancho Maxwell to the Canadian River. There was little water between here and the Cimmaron. There would be much buffalo grass and flat land. Las Vegas was a white settlement at the edge of the mountains. Mostly Spanish sheep herders lived there. Tosahwi had told Jedidiah that they did not bother the Spanish sheep herders, and they did not bother the Comanche. Same with the Apache. If the Apache find you, they will kill you. It will take a long time for you to die.

Jedidiah took two more days to heal. By then, he had finished eating the antelope. He still hurt some but thought he could ride if he took it slow and easy. A lot of time had passed, and he was sure to be far behind the brothers now. It would be some time before he would be able to ride hard and catch up.

Jedidiah saddled Goliath after breaking camp. It was well after daybreak, and he rode easy to the southwest. He was leaving known water for a dry hostile land. His canteens were full, and he had drunk his fill before leaving. What water he had, he would share with Goliath. By noon, he was worn out and found a likely place to rest for a time. He had been winding through the mountains on a trail that went along a pass. He found a gully along the western slope of the mountains on the east side of the pass. There were some trees along that slope which would provide some shade. He unsaddled Goliath and rubbed him down then gave him some water. He took one small swig for himself from the canteen. He would have to be cautious with the water now. He rested for a few hours and rode on till late that night. He had shot a rabbit along the way which he cooked that night.

Before dawn the next morning, Jedidiah was riding and stopped around noon for a few hours. He was gaining strength, but slowly. That night he cooked some of the beans with a little jerky in the pot to add flavor. He was only two days into a five-day trail to the nearest known water. He was also aware that he needed more meat but that he should not be using a gun, as the sound traveled too far and might draw attention to some wandering Apache. Overnight, he set out a few snares. The next morning, he had caught another rabbit. It was meat but it wasn't beef or venison.

Each day Jedidiah was able to ride further. On the fourth night he caught a pheasant in his snare. This was a welcome treat. He had learned to like their meat. He found some wild garlic and cooked it with the pheasant. The water, though, was nearly half gone. If he didn't find water or make it to the Cimarron River, he would run out. He had no doubt that neither he nor Goliath would last long without the water. He rode all day long without stopping on the fifth day. He saw no sign that he was getting close to that river. He knew he had been traveling slower than expected and it would be at least another day before he might get to the Cimmaron River. He now had only a little over one canteen with water. He wondered what he would do if he found it dry.

Having not caught anything in his snare that night, Jedidiah had some coffee and jerky before breaking camp. He saddled up and started riding before dawn. He traveled southwest all day. As the sun was setting in the west, he came upon the canyon. He could see a river flowing in the bottom. He rode along looking for a way down and spooked up a mule deer. He drew his six gun and dropped the deer. He replaced the bullet as he looked around. After cutting off the best parts of meat, he hung them from his saddle. Goliath wasn't too pleased with this and bucked a little twisting his head around. He found a trail down and was soon letting Goliath drink from the river. He rode along a short distance till he found a good place to camp.

Jedidiah could tell Goliath was as tired as he, so he rubbed his loyal steed down and staked him out where there was some good grass. There wasn't much along the trail. He then built a fire and began cooking the venison. He had put on a pot of coffee while the meat was cooking. As the meat was finished cooking, he ate his fill. He could see Goliath grazing contentedly while he ate. The next morning, he caught some fish out of the river. He cooked them and had them for breakfast. It was midmorning before the sun reached down into the canyon. His camp was well up from the river in some trees along the east wall of the canyon. He let Goliath rest another day but got up before dawn the next morning. From what he had been told, Las Vegas was two days' ride from here. There should be another river about a day away in that direction.

Riding across the river and up a ravine out of the canyon, Jedidiah stopped Goliath as his head rose up out of the canyon. He looked around and then eased forward cautiously. The trail was difficult all day with one canyon after another. Then he had to go around a mountain. An hour before sunset, he came to another large canyon. He rode along it a short distance looking for a way down. He didn't see any water till he was halfway down and rounding a bend. Once down, he realized this was the Mora River that he had been told about. He found a place to camp. Since it wasn't dark, he took care of Goliath and tried fishing. He caught two and enjoyed them with some coffee.

Goliath had rested and drank his fill of water and ate well from the grass along the river. Jedidiah left the river at dawn toward Las Vegas. He rode all day long without stopping. He was soon away from the low ridges and canyons and into a dry barren flatland. It was hot but easy riding; he had a good time. The sun was low just above the mountains to the west as he saw the first buildings he had seen in many days. Thinking to himself, *this had to be Las Vegas town.* Jedidiah rode around and crossed a river just north of town. Circling around and riding into town from the west and the setting sun allowed Jedidiah to enter town with the sun at his back. He preferred it this way if he was to meet one of the outlaws on the street. There was a central square, and as he rode in, people stared at him. Some townsfolk pointed at him. He did not see a sheriff's office, so he rode up to a cantina. He went inside and ordered a beer. After paying, he asked about a group of men who were coming this way. He then told them he was looking for two of them that had raped and killed his sister.

Jedidiah was told by the bar keeper that the men were there four days before and they had stolen many sheep. They went north toward Colorado, probably to sell them there. They were three days ahead of him as they were staying one more night before they drove the sheep north. He went to a stable and took care of Goliath. Then he got some beans and tortillas to eat. He found a place to sleep for the night. As he cleaned up, he was thinking if he had gone straight west, he might have caught them. He did not know at the time that the outlaws would go that way from here. At least he was a little closer now. With them moving sheep, he would have a better chance of catching them. What he would be able to do against so many guns, he wasn't sure. The people here told him that they had over thirty gunmen traveling together. He was also told that the patron here was contacting the US Army about the bad men. The patron upon hearing about the new stranger in town had some of his men hold him in a storage building. Once the army officer arrived the next day they could determine if he might be one of the bandits. Before dawn the army rode into town from Fort Union. After talking to Jedidiah, the officer was convinced that he was not part of the robbers associated with Captain Coe's gang.

As the sun came up Jedidiah was going north. He had been told by the officer that if he followed the edge of the mountains, he would find water. He was also told about a ranchero on the Cimmaron three days' ride north of here. The bad men were sure to go by there. He wasn't far out of town when he picked up their trail. It was hard to miss with that many men moving so many sheep. He made camp that night on the side of a small mountain with a fresh spring.

Jedidiah was awake before dawn eating breakfast. He had restocked his supplies in Las Vegas, including plenty of coffee. As soon as the sun was up and he could see the tracks, he followed the herd north. He was able to travel faster than the herd and was surely gaining on them. When he stopped the next night, he was certain that he was closer to them. The droppings from the sheep and the horses were fresher. He rode all day the third day without catching them. Jedidiah came to the Cimmaron River where there was a large, nice ranchero. There was also a mill, a store, and a few houses. He stopped to ask about the men driving sheep north. He was told they went by a little before noon that day. He asked if any of them had seen two men named Jake and George Allister. He described them the best he could. One old man told him that they separated from the others and went west to Elizabeth town. They said they had enough of stinking sheep and that they didn't expect to get enough from this adventure to be worth their time. Jedidiah smiled thinking he might soon get his chance at them.

Jedidiah asked about the trail west to Elizabeth Town. He was told that it was only about twenty miles if he went straight there. He would have to follow the river though. It was the only way through the mountains. The river twisted back and forth through that pass. That twenty miles would end up being thirty-five or forty miles. Once he came out from the narrow pass he would enter a small valley. The river came from the north. He needed to turn north up the valley about five miles, and then he would come to Elizabeth Town. It would be on the west side of the river with the gold digs in the mountain west of there.

They asked him if he was going chasing the men or gold. He told them he wanted those two men and explained why. Before finding a place to spend the night, he went into a cantina. He ate a meal of beans and tortillas, along with a beer. While he waited for the food a young girl sat with him smiling and talking with him. He enjoyed her company, and they talked together till late that night. Jedidiah slept in the little settlement before going west. He had been advised to only ride through that pass during daylight. If he didn't make it before dark, he would camp overnight in the pass. He was also advised that if he did camp, to do so high up above the river. A heavy rain high up in the mountains could cause a flash flood even if it didn't rain where he was.

Chapter 8: Boom Town

Jedidiah rose early and found a place to eat breakfast. After placing the saddle on Goliath, he rode out to the west. From here, he could see mountains, but he couldn't really see what lay ahead. The trail soon narrowed along the river. The mountains rose steeply on either side. With every mile traveled, the mountains seemed to get higher. At times, he would have to cross the river to follow the trail then. By noon, he passed the first small valley that they had told him about. It wasn't long before the sun sank below the peaks surrounding him. The trail narrowed, and at times, he had to ride midstream.

All too soon the sky darkened, and he decided it would be best if he looked for a place to camp. On the south side of the river, he spotted a ravine going up between two rises. Along the west side of the ravine there was a shelf he was able to ride to, which was somewhat sheltered. As he came to it, there was a rumbling in the distance and flashes over the tops of the peaks to the northwest. Jedidiah made camp with a shelter then he staked Goliath out where there was some grass.

Jedidiah walked down to the river and filled the one canteen he had used. A young buck walked nearby and he shot it. After dressing it out he carried it to his camp. It took four trips for him to get it all there. Once he had a fire started, he cooked enough meat to eat. He hung the rest over the fire after seasoning it to smoke and dry it. It would take till morning to cure but would make plenty of meat to last for some time. After his meal was cooked, he placed green wood from an oak to make plenty of smoke going up through the rest of the venison.

As full darkness came, Jedidiah was fast asleep under his shelter with his head on the saddle. Hours later a loud awakened him from his slumber. Everything around him was dry so he checked on Goliath. The horse was good, and the stars were shining. It was a full moon high in the sky lighting the pass well. He walked down toward the river to find it high and rolling. The entire bottom was a rolling torrent wide and deep. There was no sign that it had rained that he could see. Thinking to himself, *there must have been a downpour upriver, in the high mountains.*

Jedidiah got up an hour later than normal for him. He checked on Goliath; his horse seemed happy. After he started the fire and put on some coffee, Jedidiah walked to the river. It was down some but still too high for him to go through the pass. Once he looked around, he could find no other way out of the ravine. The river would have to go back down to normal flow before he could leave. At least he had plenty of meat and supplies. Later, he led Goliath down to the edge of the river and let him drink his fill of water. He found a fresh place to stake him out to graze.

***

Jake and George Allister left Captain Coe's outfit at the ranchero. Jake was sick of the sheep after one day.

Taking them to Colorado to sell did not look to be that profitable. They had heard about the gold boom at Elizabeth Town and while they were this close, they quit the outlaw band. Riding west through the pass, the two traveled toward the boomtown. That night, they stopped in the first valley as the sun sat early in the canyon pass. Midafternoon the next day, they rode into Elizabeth Town. The town had three saloons, a livery, an assayer's office, and a hotel, which wasn't more than a large tent. Two of the saloons had few rooms on the second floor. They went into the first saloon and stood at the bar. They still had a little money left from the railroad robbery, but not much. The bartender asked if they were new in town. Jake told him yes and that they were looking for gold. He told them that most of the first mountain was already full of claims. The next one across the little valley was open though. One man, Herbert, had started panning the creek and was showing a little color.

The next morning, the two brothers bought pans and equipment for gold digging with the last of their money. They rode up the mountain past Herbert's claim and staked out their location. Both of them panned all day and came up with a small amount. The two had no intention of laboring at digging for gold. Jake had a much faster plan to acquire enough gold to set them up. George would stay on the claim and work it at his leisure. He had food and plenty of whisky to occupy him till Jake was ready.

Jake headed back to town to look for a poker game. He was much better with the cards than George. Mostly, he was going to listen around to find out who was getting the gold and where it was going. His plan was to steal the gold when the opportunity arose.

Jake won more than he lost. Even so, he hadn't taken enough to draw attention to himself. One man was beginning to wonder why he was always in the saloon while his partner was up on the mountain working their claim.

Jake was at the poker table with a pile of money in front of him when the little man walked in.

****

The river had finally gone down enough that Jedidiah was sure he could make it through the pass. He had been in his camp for two and a half days. Both he and his horse were well rested and ready for anything. As soon as it was light enough to see, Jedidiah was up eating breakfast. He saddled Goliath and rode up the river.

Early in the afternoon, Jedidiah rode into Elizabeth Town. He began looking for the sheriff's office. He quickly learned that they had no lawmen here. Jedidiah asked a man on the street about Jake and George Allister. The man wouldn't say anything, but he did look toward one of the saloons. Jedidiah climbed down his rope ladder off of Goliath and as he did so, he heard a few laughs. He was used to this and let it pass as he tied his horse to a post.

Jedidiah loosed the throng off his gun and checked the load. As he walked to the saloon Jedidiah's eyes darted back and forth across the front of the building the man had looked at.. Inside, Jedidiah spotted a man at the poker table near the rear of the saloon who looked like the description of Jake Allister. Looking around, he did not see anyone that looked like the brother, George.

Jedidiah looked right at Jake and said, "Jake Allister, I'm taking you in for rape and murder."

Everyone except for Jake jumped back away from the line of fire. Jake jumped up and pulled at his gun in one motion. He hadn't cleared leather when the room was filled with the roar of a gun and smoke. Jake was shot in the center of his forehead blasting him backward over a table, his hand still on his gun. Everyone else looked at the little man, amazed at his speed.

Jedidiah asked the three men closest to him to write down what had happened so he could collect the bounty. Someone asked if he was a bounty hunter. He told them no, he had just been after the four men who raped and killed his sister.

"This is the third one I've caught up with," Jedidiah said. "Three are dead with one to go." Then he asked if anyone knew where George might be found. He hadn't noticed that one man saddled up and rode out west in a hurry. Another man told Jedidiah that George had been staying on their claim on the mountain just west of here. Jedidiah collected the statements and climbed into the saddle. Riding out of Elizabeth Town, he went west and up the mountain.

***

Herbert had gone into town for a few supplies and a drink. He was standing at the bar when a little man walked in and faced down Jake. Herbert had never seen such a fast draw as the little man. Jake Allister was dead for sure, so he slipped out of the saloon and rode west. Herbert went on past his claim and found George.

Herbert told him all about the little man and that Jake was dead. "Someone was sure to tell the little man where to find you."

Wasting no time, George grabbed a few things, saddled hastily, and lit a shuck off the mountain. In his spare time, he had roamed around some looking for signs of more gold and hunting. On one such trip, he found a pass that skirted the valley and went south and west. He had heard of a larger town south of here called Santa Fe.

****

Riding up the mountain he stopped to ask a man about George. The man said his name was Herbert and Goerge and Jake's claim was higher up the mountain. Jedidiah found the claim, but he could tell that George had left in a hurry. Going back down the mountain, Jedidiah stopped and asked Herbert about George. Herbert told him that George rode out in a hurry after he had told George about a gunman killing his brother.

Jedidiah said, "You know I'm the one who killed Jake."

"Yes, but the boys never did anything to me, and I don't know you," Herbert replied.

"They and two others raped and killed my sister, and I been tracking them ever since."

Herbert told him he did not know anything about that. If he had, he wouldn't have helped George. Herbert then told him, "There are two trails, each going around Scully Mountain. They both came together in the bigger valley right where the pass from the ranchero entered the valley."

Jedidiah went back to Elizabeth Town to get more information. He got there just in time to learn that George had stopped long enough to claim Jake's things. He left enough gold for two men to bury his brother. George then rode off to the south.

Jedidiah asked for the best route to go to Santa Fe. Herbert had told him that George might go there.

One man told him, "The only reasonable route to Santa Fe is where the river turns east through the pass. There, you'll see another pass going south. It's the fastest way down to Las Vegas. From Las Vegas, follow the Santa Fe trail west through the mountain pass. It's the easy route; the wagon trains and the stagecoaches use it. A new express route is going through there also." The man went on to say that Pony Express delivered messages from the east coast to the west in days and that two of the men involved were Buffalo Bill Cody and Kit Carson.

Jedidiah smiled and said, "I know Cody."

To that statement everyone looked at him with wonder. *What kind of man was this little guy? Such a fast draw and he says he knows Buffalo Bill Cody.* Jedidiah had already inspected the so-called hotel and decided he would prefer to sleep on the trail. He gathered a few supplies and rode out. Not far south out of town, he picked up the tracks of Georges' horse. At the point of the river going east, he noticed that the tracks went south. He followed, knowing now that this was supposed to be the fastest way back to Las Vegas.

He followed the trail south through the valley and a short pass, coming to a fork in a small meadow. The trail went south but what looked like another pass went east. One of the men in the saloon had told him that a shorter route went that way, but the trail went the longer way. He thought of taking the shorter route and cutting George off; but decided not to since George might stop, change directions, and even turn back. Following the trail into the pass, he camped along a creek flowing from the pass back to the Cimmaron River. There was a stream flowing off a mountain to the creek and it looked to be loaded with trout. After taking care of Goliath, he fixed camp and went fishing. After catching two, he cleaned them and cooked them along with a pot of coffee. After eating, he slept well. By first light, he was on the trail watching for tracks.

The next morning, he followed the trail into the pass going south. At times, he could see the tracks left by George Allister. By midmorning, he came to a large meadow. George's tracks were looking older and looked like he was pushing his horse hard and fast. He was on the run, of that Jedidiah was sure. Though he thought there might be an easier way out to the east and then south, Jedidiah followed the tracks into the pass going straight south. The trail wound around a narrow steep pass with mountains rising up on either side. Going straight through might only be five miles, but following the trail was over ten.

Jedidiah came out of the pass into a long narrow valley. It was a mile wide and fourteen miles long. Since it was late afternoon and the sun was behind the mountains, he looked for a campsite. At the head of the valley, he found a small hill next to the creek which flowed through the pass and valley. There were some trees on the hill which would make for a good campsite. He watered Goliath in the creek before going up the hill. After he built a fire and put on some coffee, he went back down to the creek and caught some trout. Tonight, and tomorrow morning, he will eat well. As night came on, he thought he could hear sounds drifting from the south. It sounded like noise from a town. If so, it was a long way off. Most likely he will find out tomorrow.

Waking up early, he ate and saddled up to hit the trail south. By noon, he was riding into a town. *This must have been what I heard last night,* he thought. It was a small Spanish village with a cantina, a store, a church, and a livery stable all around a square. It was on the south side of a river that the creek he had been following flowed into. He saw the name Mora, and he did not see a sheriff's office. *Law hasn't reached here either*, he thought. Riding up to the cantina, he climbed off Goliath, then went inside. He looked around for a man that looked like George. Seeing only Mexican or Spanish-looking men, he went to the end of the bar as the weight of everyone's eyes followed him closely. From beside the bar, he asked for a beer. After paying for the beer, he walked to a table and sat down. Sitting with his back to a wall, he took a long drink, then asked if anyone had seen a white man with a scar in the last two days. No one said anything. He then told them that he was after the last man who had raped and killed his sister. One man began speaking Spanish to the rest. Jedidiah took hold of one or two words, enough to get the idea he was telling them what he had said. Another man then said something to the first.

After that, the first man spoke to Jedidiah in English. "Yes, this man came through yesterday. He left this morning going to Santa Fe. He had asked for the shortest way there and fastest. He was told the shortest is up and over the mountains. There was a trail that some have traveled through. Many have tried though, but most were never seen from again. It is very high up, for every step you go west, you must go a step higher. There is always snow up there, and it is very cold. There are wolves and many grizzlies which are very big and mean. Cougars are up there also. This late in the summer they will be hungry. They say there is much gold up there, but nobody has brought it out yet. The man would only hear which way was closest. Santa Fe is the same distance as Las Vegas, if you could go straight, which is impossible. He is a very determined man; perhaps he will make it through. It will be very difficult though."

Jedidiah rode out to the west and found George's tracks. He followed them for two hours and could tell that what the Mexican had told him was right, but George had gone that way. He returned to Mora just before sunset. He placed Goliath in the stable and got a place for himself. The next day, he would take the longer route around Santa Fe. When he had been to Las Vegas before, he had shown them the "wanted" poster of the four men, and they said they would pass it on down the trail.

Chapter 9: The Santa Fe Trail

Jedidiah woke up early and ate breakfast at the cantina. He then saddled Goliath and rode out to the southeast. By noon, he was back out on the east edge of the mountains going south towards Las Vegas. He knew from here it was two easy days to the Spanish town, so he rode slow. Goliath seemed to appreciate the slower pace; it had been a long journey since they had left home.

The ride to Las Vegas was uneventful. Jedidiah placed Goliath in the stable and checked into a room for himself. He then went to the cantina for a beer and to catch up on the talk. He learned that a small wagon train had passed through two days earlier. He also learned that an army patrol had been there from Fort Union that morning. They had informed the town that the Apache had been stirred up by the band of outlaws led by Captain Coe. The main force from the fort had gone after Coe and his band. The small patrol was going to catch up with the wagon train and escort them through to Santa Fe. Jedidiah figured it might be wise if he caught up with the wagon train and rode with them west. He got up early and saddled Goliath. Together they rode west at a rapid pace. After a good night and two days of easy riding, Goliath was ready for a fast-paced ride.

A lone man on horseback could travel twice as fast as a wagon train. Riding hard, he could see the light from their fires just as the sun was setting. Riding up close he announced his presence. A man he couldn't see answered him. Jedidiah told them he was riding west to Santa Fe, and they had told him about the wagon train and patrol in Las Vegas. He had ridden as fast as he could all day to catch up with them. They told him he could come on into the camp. As he entered, he saw that the man talking to him was the army officer.

Upon seeing the little man on the large Morgan horse, Army Lieutenant Jason Bell recognized who he was. They had been advised about him and his objective.

The lieutenant walked with Jedidiah to the wagon master. Jedidiah asked, "may I ride along with the wagon train to Santa Fe? I heard in Las Vegas about the Apache and thought it would be best if I had some company going through." He then told the wagon master he could offer his gun. The lieutenant told the wagon master that he had heard that his gun was fast and true. The wagon master told him he was welcome and that he could put his things by his fire. His cook had food ready, and he was welcomed to all he could eat. They had good jackrabbit stew and plenty of hot coffee.

It was later than he would normally be traveling before the wagon train began to move. Jedidiah quickly learned their pace and system. He made himself useful by riding off to the side and forward of the train. He stayed below the top of the rises, but high enough he could see over them and as far as possible around. His efforts were noticed not only by the wagon master but by the army as well. This being a heavily traveled portion of the Santa Fe trail, it was well beaten down. There were few obstacles to stop or slow the wagons.

By midday, a cloud of dust rose from their rear. The army patrol and Jedidiah moved to the rear of the train. Jedidiah rode back a little further and turned up a rise to see around a slight bend. He went to the lieutenant and told him that it looked like a stagecoach coming up fast. The lieutenant sent one man forward to tell the wagon master. He rode back telling each wagon and asked them to push as far to the right as they could and allow the stage to pass them on the left.

The stage slowed slightly as the lieutenant and wagon master rode alongside to talk. The stagecoach driver hadn't seen anything since leaving Las Vegas. He was pushing as hard as he could on to the station, midway from Las Vegas to Santa Fe. His plan was to spend the night at the station and make Santa Fe the next night.

The next morning, they were moving again. In the afternoon they began seeing smoke rising from the trail ahead. The Lieutenant rode up next to the wagon master. Seeing this, Jedidiah rode up to them also. They both figured that it was the stagecoach station burning. The Lieutenant told them that his orders were to stay with the train till they reached Santa Fe. Then he said he would send out a man to scout ahead if he needed to.

The wagon master told him that he had a trained scout out there already. "He should be coming back this way to tell us what happened soon enough."

They hadn't even finished talking when the scout came riding in hard and fast. He told them that it was the station burning along with the shed. He had an arrow to show them, and it was Apache. He told them there was no one left alive there. The stagecoach was also burning, and the horses were all gone. The wagon master said that it was typical of Apache that they wouldn't leave the horses. He then told the scout to exchange his horse with one from the remuda, then ride back out to watch for any sign. He told him not to go too far and not to take any chances.

Jedidiah rode back out a short distance paralleling the train at a place he could see as far as possible. He watched Goliath and looked all around. They swung wide around the station so that the people wouldn't have to look at the devastation. A few of the men rode ahead before the train got there and buried the dead. There was the stagecoach driver, two unknown passengers, and the station keeper. They found the mail pouch charred but the insides were still intact. The pouch was given to the lieutenant to deliver.

It took three more days for the wagon train to get to Santa Fe. None of them ever saw an Apache. The Apache raiding party saw them though. They followed the train for a short distance only looking over a ridge at a point that they could watch through some scrub brush. This allowed them to see without being seen. They were a small band and had already taken many horses. They had lost two warriors but taken four scalps. Seeing the soldiers and many heavily armed riders, they decided to let this wagon train go on, for now.

The wagon train came into Santa Fe. The town seemed to empty out to greet them. It was an old town and one of fair size. They had a marshal, and Jedidiah went to see him. The lieutenant and the wagon master beat him there. They were telling him about the stage and the station. The marshal told them that it was bad, and that he knew the driver, Curly. "He was a good ace," the marshal said. "Though he didn't have a family that I knew of."

The Lieutenant gave the marshal the mail pouch, and the marshal said, "I'll take it to the office for them to sort it out. "He then looked at Jedidiah and asked, "You are Jedidiah, aren't you? I've been waiting and watching for you." He then explained that the poster on the four men had gotten to him and the next day, this half-dead man rode in from the north matching one of their descriptions. Jedidiah told him he would look at him and identify him if it was.

They went into the jail and in a cell at the back sat George. Jedidiah asked him if he remembered the girl back in Missouri.

George said, "So it's you. Are you going to kill me here in the jail cell?"

Jedidiah told him he wouldn't do that. He told him, "I shot Brody and Jake, though, and I watched Lester hang. That is what I'm going to do here. I will wait till there's a trial. I will testify about what you and the others did. Then I will watch them hang you." Jedidiah asked the marshal if that would work for him. The marshal told him that was what he had been waiting for. He would get word to the circuit judge to set the trial as soon as he could. If George was found guilty, they would begin erecting gallows. Then on the set time and day, they would carry out the sentence.

Jedidiah told the wagon master and the lieutenant that he would be staying on in Santa Fe for some time. The lieutenant told them he was going to wait for the east bound stage and escort it back to Las Vegas. Then he would be going back to Fort Union. "Once I make my report, we might be mounting an offensive against the Apache," Lieutenant Jason Bell said. "It depends on how well the campaign against Captain Coe goes."

Jedidiah told him that Coe had thirty to forty hardened men with him and was probably back in his fortress on Robber Roost. The lieutenant told them that the colonel going out after him had a hundred troops along with two artillery pieces. "If he has to, he will blast the fortress into the ground," Lieutenant Bell said. "Jedidiah, do you want to go back to Las Vegas with our men?

Jedidiah said, "No, I am staying here till the trial."

Jedidiah put Goliath in the livery stable and asked the proprietor to take exceptional care of him. He then carried all his things to the hotel down the street from the jail. He checked in and was given a room overlooking the street. The front desk recommended the café down the street. Inside, he ordered a steak with all the fixings. It had been a long time, back in Dodge, since he had tasted beef. With the last man caught and in jail, he began thinking about the future and what he would do. He thought of Buffalo Bill Cody and his offer. He just might have to find him and see if that offer still stood. He finished his meal and went to his room.

After eating breakfast the next morning, Jedidiah walked the street. He liked this place. It was peaceful and beautiful. Santa Fe sat right at the foot of mountains to the east. Fifteen miles west, the Rio Grande flowed out of the mountains, going south. Another five miles west of there were more mountains, with a large open pass south of them. The Santa Fe trail went in that direction from here and on to California. It was a nice day also and the people were friendly. No one had called him Shorty or laughed at him. He looked up to see the wagon master coming his way. Jedidiah told him he thought they would have left by now. The wagon master told him this would be their last chance to get supplies and rest up for a long time. They were getting extra barrels and filling them with water. He then told Jedidiah that they would be pulling out first thing tomorrow morning.

The marshal caught up with Jediah before he got back to the hotel and told him that he had talked to the judge. The trial was set for the day after tomorrow starting at ten o'clock. He also told him that they had checked the bounty on George and was giving it to Jedidiah. If he went to the bank, they were expecting him and would get the money for him. Jedidiah told the marshal he wasn't the one who captured George, but the marshal could not accept bounties. Therefore, the bounty belonged to Jedidiah.

Jedidiah went to the jail and asked if he could talk to George. He had to leave his guns in the office then was escorted back to see the prisoner. He looked at George sitting alone, looking weak and beaten in the jail cell and asked him, "Why did you do that to my sister?"

George sat there looking at him for a while then explained. "It was Jake's idea. He was always starting things, and I would go along with it Seemed like it was always getting worse and worse. Though that was the worst thing that I even knew of us doing. She was so pretty and innocent."

Jedidiah cursed him saying, "You took the only family I had" before he left the jail and went to the cantina. He drank two beers before returning to his room.

Jedidiah walked the streets of Santa Fe the next day. He thought about George and what he had said about Jake. George had remorse about what he had done. If he displayed that at the trial, he might get some leniency. How did he feel about that? Thinking it over, he figured if the law could be merciful and sentence him to life in prison, then he would be okay with it. With that realization, he felt relief, like a load was lifted from him. From the night he first learned about his sister's death till now it had been over two years. Most of that time was him getting what he needed to go after the outlaws and practicing with his gun. Then almost a year tracking them down. He wasn't sure what they had done for so long around Kansas City. Once the "wanted" posters went out and he started after them, they had moved fairly rapidly west. They left a trail of crime as they went.

Jedidiah went into the café to eat. A little later, a man came in and looked around. He was wearing buckskins that were painted and fancy with leather fringe all along the sleeves. He carried two bone handled pistols each hung low on his legs and tied down. He looked right at Jedidiah and came to his table.

"May I sit with you?" he asked. Jedidiah told him OK and as he sat down, he told him, "I'm Kit Carson. I heard about you from a mutual friend, Bill Cody."

Jedidiah said to Carson, "My task is about to be over, and I am thinking about the offer that Cody had made me."

Carson replied, "I know Cody will honor the offer to you if you want to go with him. Cody would probably be somewhere around Kansas City for some time. He was trying to put together that wild west show he has been talking about for so long."

Jedidiah told Carson that as soon as the trial was over tomorrow and then the hanging, he would be free to go. He then asked about the Apache and that situation. Carson told him he had been out scouting around and was sure that it was a band of young bucks out to make a name for themselves. He thought it would settle down now for a while, and the stages should be operating soon enough. He told Jedidiah that he could catch a stage here and be in Kansas City in a little over a week. Jedidiah told him he had a great horse that he wouldn't leave behind. They had been through a lot together.

Kit told him, "I can't blame you there ain't nothing more important out here than a trusted horse, except honor. You can tell a lot about a man's honor by how he cares for his horse."

Jedidiah told him that he would ride back east as soon as this ordeal was finished, but he had to see it out. He then told him that he didn't know how long it would be before they hung George if they found him guilty. Kit told him it wouldn't be long as they could put the gallows up in a day. It was only partially apart and stored in the warehouse behind the government building. There was a courtroom in the government building and that was where the trial would be. He then told Jedidiah he would be here at least two more days on business then he would be going through Las Vegas to Fort Union. If it works out, we can ride together there. I can make arrangements for you to ride along with a supply wagon going from the fort to the end of the line on the train in Kansas. You can get passage for you and your horse on a train going to Kansas City. "Think about it and let me know." Said Kit Carson "I'd be pleased to have you along."

Jedidiah went to his room, gathered his best clothes, and went to a laundry he had found on the next street. His clothes would be cleaned and delivered to his room in the morning. He went back to his room and cleaned up before heading to eat.

The next morning, his clean clothes were at his door. He put them on and went out to eat breakfast. He checked on Goliath who seemed pleased to see him. He looked good and showed signs of good care. From there, Jedidiah went to the government house and found his way to the courtroom. A deputy was standing guard at the door and hung Jedidiah's gun on a peg across the hall. After that, the deputy allowed him in, recognizing him as a witness.

It was thirty minutes before the marshal led George out wearing leg irons and a chain threaded to his handcuffs. George hung his head low as he passed by Jedidiah. George was seated on the judge's right side of the aisle at a table with two chairs. The marshal sat right behind him. The prosecuting attorney came in and sat at a table on the judge's left side of the room. Several other people began coming in and the courtroom was at ten o'clock. A deputy shouted, "All rise," and then announced the judge. Once the judge had sat down, the deputy told everyone to sit down and be quiet. The prosecutor read a list of charges against George Allister. Jedidiah was surprised to hear the robberies and cattle rustling were also added to the charges. Then the judge read "rape and murder of a young innocent girl." The judge then looked at George and asked him how he pleaded.

George asked, "What does that even mean, judge?"

With a sigh, the judge asked, "Are you guilty of these crimes and agree to admit it at this time? If so, I can pronounce the sentence, and the trial will be over."

George thought about it for a minute. He hoped for compassion and admitted to all the crimes. The judge asked the prosecutor if he had anything to add. The prosecutor said that the witness should be allowed to tell the jury and the judge about the crime against his sister. The judge agreed and asked Jedidiah to come up.

He was sworn in and allowed a statement in his own words. Jedidiah looked first at George then at the jury. With tears beginning to show in his eyes he said, "George Allister and the other three men robbed and killed my friend. Then they came into town and followed my sister into the street from work. They pushed her into an alley, each one raped her before killed her. One of them had used a knife and slit her throat." With the tears flowing freely stated, "Our parents had died years before, my sister was all I had. She had been taking care of me. He then told the judge that he had talked with George in the jail, and he believed that George had remorse for his actions. Jedidiah said, "Since his brother was dead and he admitted his crimes, maybe life in prison would be enough punishment."

The judge then asked Jedidiah to return to his seat. He told the jury that since the defendant had pleaded guilty, their service would not be necessary. The judge looked at some papers, then looked around the room. He looked right at Jedidiah and asked George to stand up. Looking George right in the eyes, he said, "New Mexico does not have a penitentiary at this date. If we did, I might have sentenced you to a life of hard labor. Therefore, you are sentenced to hang by the neck until dead. Sentence is to be carried out at noon the day after tomorrow. Marshal, you are tasked with putting the gallows up and contacting the hangman. You will keep the prisoner secure in your jail till it is time for the sentence to be carried out." With a loud gasp George lowered his head down to the desk, as his body trembled all over.

Jedidiah went to see George in jail the next morning after the trial. He stood at the window watching the gallows go up and told Jedidiah that he wished he had died up on the high mountain. "It would have been easier than watching them build the gallows to hang me," George said. He then told Jedidiah the thing that he regretted the most was what they had done to his sister. He then asked what her name was.

Jedidiah said, "Jessica." He then added, "I tried to speak up for you while telling the truth of it."

George told him he heard that and appreciated it. They talked a little longer, then Jedidiah went back to the hotel. Kit was in the lobby as he walked in. Kit told him that he would finish up his business the next day and would be going to Las Vegas the day after.

Jedidiah told him he would be ready and would ride with him all the way to the fort.

Chapter 10: The Way Back

Jedidiah watched as George was led to the gallows. He saw the judge nod his head and heard the trap door drop open. George dropped with the door and never kicked; he just hung there. He looked at the last of the four men who had killed his sister for a moment longer, then he turned to go back to his hotel room.

He began packing his belongings and checking his supplies. He then went to the store to buy what he needed for the trail back east. Jedidiah went to the stable and told the owner he would be leaving early the next morning and settled his bill for the care of Goliath. He packed the supplies in the bags he would place on Goliath's back. Then he went to the cantina. The bartender was used to seeing him and brought a beer to the table.

Later, Kit Carson came in, looked around, and sat at the table with Jedidiah. Kit told Jedidiah that he would be ready to ride at first light in the morning. Jedidiah told him he would be saddled and ready. They drank another beer, then Jedidiah went back to his room.

Sunrise the next morning revealed Jedidiah and Kit riding southeast on the trail to Las Vegas. Jedidiah looked back as they rounded a bend thinking he would like to come back here someday. He liked Santa Fe; it was a pretty town with friendly folk. He wondered about the trip back to

Kansas City. It was bound to be a long hard trip, but he hoped it wouldn't be as dangerous as the trip out here. That made him rub the scar on his left abdomen. They rode all day till the sun was setting. They stopped at the stagecoach station for the night. There were men there that had been rebuilding the station. They were building it bigger and stronger with shooting slits instead of windows. It was made of adobe instead of wood. The corral was behind the station house in some shrubs and up against the rise of the mountain. It looked much easier to defend.

They rode on to Las Vegas the next morning. Along the way, they met a wagon of supplies and some men driving horses to the station. The station should be up and running again the next day. They might not be finished with the house, but it would be operational. They spent the night in Las Vegas before starting toward Fort Union the next day. It was a day's ride northeast across two rivers by what Kit told Jedidiah. One of the rivers was the Mora, which came out of the mountains past the town Mora. They crossed the rivers and came to the fort. It was on the east side of Wolf Creek and about three miles southwest of Turkey Mountain.

Fort Union had a three-story adobe guard house on the northwest corner. Two story tall wood barricades surrounded the fort. There was a large gate, and he could see another adobe guard house on the opposing corner of the fort. As they rode inside, Jedidiah could see a large wood building. There was a trading post in the building as well as the officers' quarters. To the left were the troopers' quarters and on the right were the horse stables. He could see at least four cannons. The roof of the large trading post building was the tallest point of the fort. On its roof, a menacing-looking gatling gun set at the ready, along with three troopers.

Jedidiah waited four days in Fort Union before a pair of wagons left going east. Along with them was a six-man patrol. Their destination was Fort Dodge. Jedidiah was soon on his way back to Dodge. This time he was with an army patrol with a wagon carrying plenty of water and food. One of the teamsters was reported to be a good cook and would prepare their meals.

Jedidiah talked with Lieutenant James who was in charge of the patrol. He asked about their route and was told they would go pretty much straight to Fort Dodge. It was around three hundred miles, and he hoped to make it in fifteen days. Jedidiah then asked if they were going by Robbers Roost. Lieutenant James told him yes and he had just gotten back from there. He had been a part of the men that attacked the fortress. He told Jedidiah that they had blasted the walls down with cannon fire. What few men survived, ran. They had found the body of Captain Coe. They had brought back five injured outlaws and turned them over to civilian authorities. That should be the end of that rabble.

Jedidiah then asked about Turkey Mountain by the fort. He asked if it had been a volcano and if it was a Comanche burial ground. The lieutenant told him it was an extinct volcano but not a burial ground. Jedidiah told the Lieutenant about Tosahwi and the band of Comanche that had helped him. "They were going back to the Indian territory from burying his father in the old burial grounds," Jedidiah said.

The lieutenant told him that it would be a very old cinder cone just east of Capulin Volcano. There was a protected Comanche burial ground there. "It is lucky for Tosahwi that they weren't caught in New Mexico," the lieutenant said. "They weren't supposed to leave the Oklahoma Territory."

Jedidiah told the lieutenant that they should be allowed to take a pilgrimage like this. Lieutenant James told him that he agreed, but it wasn't up to him to make such decisions.

Midday on the sixth day they came to the dry Cimmaron River. That night they camped not far from where the Comanche helped Jedidiah. The next morning, they were going past Robbers Roost. Jedidiah turned to ride up the mountain and the Lieutenant sent one of his troopers to go with him. He saw that the entire front end of the Fortress had been blasted away. The back wall had collapsed also. He rode back to catch up with the wagons. They followed the river for four days then turned straight east to the fresh water source at Seymour's homestead. They camped along the river before breaking out of the valley onto the flat. It was two and a half days to Seymour's place. It was an uneventful ride. They arrived at Seymour's in the afternoon. They watered all the stock and gave Seymour some of their supplies. Jedidiah gave him a fair amount of coffee which he remembered that Seymour liked. The troopers spent that night there before going on to Dodge. Jedidiah and they all knew there was no water to be found between here and Dodge.

They went slower on this stretch to make it easier on the horses. They had water barrels with plenty of water

for them and their stock. It would take three days to get to
Fort Dodge. The fort was just over four miles southeast of
the town. The wagons went straight to the fort passing
about a mile south of the town. Jedidiah stayed with them
till they were in the fort. He told the lieutenant goodbye and
rode back to the town of Dodge. He put Goliath in the
livery stable and went to the Dodge House. He asked for a
room and was given one on the back side this time. He put
his things away and went to the café to eat. He was eating a
steak with a cup of coffee when Wild Bill Hickok came in,
wearing a badge.

Wild Bill saw Jedidiah and sat down beside him. "I
believe you are Jedidiah. Wyatt told me about you." He
then asked about the Allister brothers.

Jedidiah told him they were both dead. He had shot
Jake and George was hung in Santa Fe. Hickok told him
that was good. Then he told Jedidiah, "You won't be
needing your gun. There is an ordinance about wearing
guns in town now." Hickok took Jedidiah's gun and told
him he could have it back when he was ready to leave
town.

After eating, Jedidiah went to the south side of town
where a train station was being built. He asked one of the
workers how far it was to the end of the line. They told him
it was this side of Hutchison but getting closer every day.
They had many men working and racing to get to the west
coast. He asked about getting a ride to Kansas City for him
and his horse. The man looked him over and said, "You're
the man who got those outlaws that robbed the payroll. I
will see that you get a free ride all the way from anywhere

you're able to catch up with the train." Jedidiah told him he would be riding that way at first light.

The next morning, Jedidiah had everything loaded onto Goliath and walked his horse to the sheriff's office. He asked for his gun, telling Hickok he was leaving town for Kansas City. He rode along the railroad bed and camped with the workers that night. He spent two nights along the railroad bed with workers getting it ready to lay track. On the third day, he could see smoke and many more workers in the distance. As he came closer, he could see flatbed cars with an engine on the other side. They were removing rails from the cars and laying them on ties across the bed. Workers were putting down ties ahead of them and they were nailing down the rails.

Jedidiah rode up to the man that looked to be in charge. He handed him the paper that the man in Dodge had given him. The man read it and said that the train would be going back to Hutchison as soon as they unloaded it. He would have to stay close and would have to ride on the flatbed with his horse. In Hutchison, he would be able to catch a train to Kansas City and would be in a passenger car. His horse would be placed in a stockcar. They had both at Hutchison. In two days, he will be in Kansas City. Jedidiah would have traveled from Santa Fe to Kansas City in twenty-two days. It had taken him close to a year going west on that route.

In Hutchison, he led Goliath off the flatbed car and down a ramp. He tied him up at the station and went inside to show them the letter. The teller read the letter and raised his eyebrow at the signature. He told Jedidiah that the train going east would be leaving at dawn. He wrote out tickets for Jedidiah, giving him passage to Kansas City. He told Jedidiah that he needed to be here, ready to get onboard before the train was ready to leave at first light.

Jedidiah went into town to eat and clean up a little. He put Goliath in the stable with feed and water, telling the owner he would be leaving before daylight. Jedidiah went to the telegraph office and sent a message to Buffalo Bill, telling him he was on his way to Kansas City. He went to the hotel and checked in.

The next morning, he led Goliath to the stock car on the train. He placed him inside and removed his bridle. He placed his luggage and saddle in the proper pile on the loading dock. He showed his ticket to the conductor as he boarded the passenger car. There was one woman with a little girl sitting together at one end of the car and a man sitting at the other end. He selected a seat in the middle facing the man. He sat with his gun hand on the aisle side of himself. A few minutes later, he felt a jerk and the train began moving northeast.

Jedidiah rode in silence all day. He looked out the window watching the miles go past and thinking about his journey west past these same locations. He heard the change in the sound of the locomotive as they crossed the bridges over the rivers. He watched as the dry country slowly changed to green. He realized how he had missed the green and the trees. By nightfall the train began to slow and they came into Emporia, Kansas. The conductor came by, telling him he might as well get off as there would be a two-hour delay as they took on water and fuel. They would then go on traveling through the night and arrive in Kansas City before noon tomorrow. Jedidiah checked on Goliath and found him okay. He promised him a sugar cube before they left again. He then went to eat. Within two hours, he was back on the train giving Goliath the sugar cube he had promised. He told Goliath that tomorrow by noon, he would be able to get off the train.

No more than an hour later, Jedidiah laid his head against the wall and fell asleep. The other man had not gotten back on the train, but an older couple had. There was also a man with a valise, who looked like a whisky drummer who carried samples to saloons, drumming up business. Jedidiah woke and stirred several times during the night. He woke up as light began shining into the passenger car. The conductor came by and offered him some coffee. He accepted with his thanks and pulled out a sweet biscuit he had brought from Emporia. This was his breakfast. He thought of Goliath but could not do anything for him till they reached Kansas City.

Four hours later the train slowed to enter Kansas City. Once it stopped, Jedidiah let the women folk get off first. As he stepped off the train, he was met by none other than a smiling Buffalo Bill Cody. "Good to see ya lad, but where is your mighty steed?" Cody asked.

Jedidiah pointed to the stock car, and they went to it to collect Goliath. Jedidiah led Goliath down the ramp and to the station luggage dock. Buffalo Bill picked up the saddle and gear, and with a swift swing, lay the saddle on Goliath's back. Jedidiah laughed and they all walked together toward town. Buffalo Bill told him he had a room reserved at the same hotel he was in. There was a good livery stable right around the corner which would take good care of Goliath.

Jedidiah saw to the care of Goliath, then went to his hotel room. Buffalo Bill told him they would meet in the lobby at six and go together for dinner to a very nice restaurant called Delmonico's. He cleaned up the best he could and was waiting for Buffalo Bill in the lobby. They walked down the street then crossed to the other side to the restaurant.

As they went inside, a doorman looked up and said, "I have a table for you Mr. Cody." They ordered steaks with all the trimmings and a bottle of wine. Buffalo Bill told Jedidiah he would take him to a store tomorrow to buy new clothes for him. "Some would be clothes for you to wear at the show. I'll get you some working clothes too," Buffalo Bill said. He then told Jedidiah that almost everything was ready, and the others were around the city. In a few days the tent would be ready, then they would set it up and begin practicing. Once they were ready, their first show would be here.

Jedidiah was in Kansas City and learning to be a showman. He was not twenty years old yet. He got the new clothing and learned what Buffalo Bill wanted him to do. It was simple. He was to ride in at a gallop on Goliath and shoot six bottles placed at different places. This would show his riding skills along with his shooting ability. Later that day, he rode Goliath out of town and tossed out six bottles. He then galloped Goliath back to the bottles and shot all six as fast as he could. He found out he would have to be very fast to get all six before Goliath rode past them. He practiced this a few more times then looked back to see Buffalo Bill sitting on a horse nearby watching him.

"You're as good as I remembered," Buffalo Bill said.

Chapter 11: The Show

The tent arrived overnight and was waiting for them on the loading dock at the train station. Buffalo Bill took his troop with a large freight wagon and loaded onto the wagon. They hauled it across the track into a shaded meadow just out of town. They unloaded the tent and began spreading it out. Once it was spread out, they started hammering down the stakes. With everyone helping, they pushed the top up using the long poles to hold it up. In an hour, they had the tent up and stretched tight. Buffalo Bill Cody marked out an arena in the middle and told them this would be where everyone would perform.

"We will need to build seating on each side for people to sit and watch," Buffalo Bill said. "We will also need a ticket booth just outside that opening for the people to come in. That opening across from it is where we will come and go as we perform the show. You each know what your act will be. Once we start practicing putting it all together, I will designate the order of the acts."

They began practice and in their spare time, they built the stands and ticket booth. After three days, Buffalo Bill Cody felt they were ready. He had handbills made at the newspaper office and placed an advertisement on the front page: *Come see the Buffalo Bill Cody Wild West Show*. The first ten people would get free, front row seating. Two hours before the show, he left with the troop all following him into town wearing their show clothes. Buffalo Bill Cody rode a buckskin horse wearing white buckskins with frills of leather hanging off his arms and legs. He wore a big white Montana-cut hat and waved as he led the parade. They circled through the city with many following them back.

The show was a success, and they played three more nights. One of the acts was an Indian maiden dancing to the beat of drums. Her name was Ayita which means "First to Dance". Once he met her, Jedidiah was smitten. She was beautiful. He was sure that she would never be interested in him, though. Every time he came near her, he could not speak. He had never truly known fear, but now he did.

Before the third show, Buffalo Bill Cody gathered them all together. He told them that they were making as much money as he had hoped for. He then told them that he was planning for them to travel to St. Louis after the last show here. He would pay them after the last show in each city. He hoped that the show would grow as the crowds and money came in. It was his intention to continue on to New York City and hopefully make a lot of money. They would travel east on railroad with box cars for their gear, stock cars for their livestock, flatcars for their freight wagons, and passenger cars for them. He then announced they had a new attraction starting tonight. He whistled loudly and Sitting Bull rode into the arena on a pony painted for war. Sitting Bull wore a full headdress of feathers and war paint. Annie Oakley, Pawnee Bill, and Texas Jack Omohundro were already a part of the show. Jedidiah was thinking this was really going to be a show worth paying for.

During the show, when Sitting Bull rode out into the area, the crowd cheered enthusiastically. He was a big hit and a surprise to the town's people. Buffalo Bill Cody had slipped him in without anyone knowing except his show crew. They finished the fourth night late.

"Get a good night's sleep," Buffalo Bill said. "We're tearing down at first light."

They had to be loaded on the train by dawn the next day. The bleachers and even the ticket booth were all made to be taken apart in sections. These sections could be moved and hauled with ease. Buffalo Bill had telegraphed ahead to hire extra help in St. Louis when they arrived, and the workers assisted with the tear-down.

It was an hour after dark before they had everything loaded and tied down on the train. The stock was all in a pen by the stock cars. They would load them an hour before the train was to leave. Since they were using so many cars, the entire train was reserved for them. Bill Cody and Jedidiah both had the clout with the railroad company to make this happen. Since it was a dedicated train for them, it went straight through to Saint Louis, traveling at top speed and would arrive before dark. A little over eight hours later, the train slowed as it came into St. Louis, Missouri. It was the first time since he left home that Jedidiah was back in his home state. Although this time, he was on the opposite side of the state.

Jedidiah had heard about St. Louis all his life but did not think he would ever see it. As they slowed coming into town, Ayita had watched him from two seats back and moved to sit beside him. She asked if this was where he was from. He told her, "This state, but not this city. I have never been here before. Where are you from?" She told him she was Cherokee and was from northeastern Oklahoma. Her people had come from Tennessee before she was born. She heard stories from her people about how hard the trail had been. Jedidiah told her she was beautiful, and he loved watching her dance. She leaned closer to him to look out the window at the buildings they were going by. Some were five stories high. She could see ladies wearing long dresses and carrying parasols. Ayita asked him what those things were that the women were carrying. "They are used to shade their heads, I guess," Jedidiah said. This was all new to him too.

Once the train stopped, they all exited, and the stock was unloaded first and put in a pen. Those who had horses, saw to their needs. The others all began unloading the train onto the wagons. As soon as they had everything on the wagons, they followed Buffalo Bill Cody to an open field at the edge of town. He left a couple men there to guard their things and told two other men to relieve those watching the gear in four hours. The rest went to a hotel to sleep. .

A little after dawn, they were all up at the field unloading the gear and setting up in the tent. They had it up and ready by midafternoon while Buffalo Bill was in town handing out flyers for the show. He had sent a telegraph to the newspaper asking for the advertisements to be made. At four in the afternoon, the crew were in costume, and Buffalo Bill led them in a parade through town.

Buffalo Bill told the troop that morning they would stay five days with two shows on Saturday, one at noon and another at six in the evening. Sunday, they would tear down and load onto the train. The same train would be on the sidetrack waiting for them. They would go from here to Chicago on Monday and unload that night.

It was Tuesday at six in the evening when the show was about to begin. The tent was packed with spectators. Buffalo Bill Cody rode in and told them what to expect. Texas Jack rode in after, twirling a rope and performing rope tricks none of them had seen before. Ayita danced to the beat of drums. As she danced out one side of the tent, a drum roll drew everyone's attention back to the other entrance. Sitting Bull rode in wearing his full regalia. Jedidiah rode in on Goliath. Everyone laughed. When he drew his gun with lightning speed and left six bottles laying scattered on the ground, the laughter stopped and was replaced with applause.

Ayita watched Jedidiah and came up with an idea. Little did Jedidiah know, she too was becoming interested in him.

After the show and everything was put away for the night, everyone walked to the hotel. Ayita walked next to Jedidiah. She said to him, "I have an idea that I could hold two bottles over my head, and you can shoot them." He did not like the idea of putting her at risk. He knew he could do it but did not want to put her in such danger.

The next day, they talked to Cody, and he loved the idea. That night, as Jedidiah galloped in on Goliath, there were only four bottles on the ground. Ayita came running toward him with two bottles, one in each hand high over her head. He shot the four on the ground and the two in her hands as he galloped past her. There were cheers with people on their feet clapping. Jedidiah's act had just evolved to the next level. It didn't go unnoticed by him either that Ayita was wearing a different costume. Instead of her usual full dance costume that went to her ankles with lots of feathers, she wore a short buckskin dress showing most of her beautiful legs. Once they were both outside and Jedidiah was off of Goliath, she hugged him. "I'm so glad you did not miss!" He told her he hated to admit it, but he was shaking, afraid he would hit her.

The show went on with a packed house with every performance. Several people came back to see it a second time. Others who heard about it, rode for miles to see the show. Saturday night after the show Buffalo Bill paid them all and told them to be here at first light to tear it all down and load the train. He then talked to Jedidiah and Ayita about an idea he had to improve their act. Ayita liked it and told him that Jedidiah could do it easily. Buffalo Bill told them he would telegraph ahead and have the needed piece built and waiting for them. They could practice while the others put the tent up. Sunday morning, they were all working to take everything down and load it on the train. The train pulled out of the yard in St Louis and headed to Chicago at dusk. Ayita sat next to Jedidiah; they talked for a while. Soon, she was asleep leaning against Jedidiah's shoulder. He pulled a blanket over her and fell asleep himself.

The show train pulled into Chicago at noon. They unloaded everything and moved it to the location for the show. Buffalo Bill Cody told them to get a good night's sleep as they would put the tent up at first light. They were to be ready for a show by six that afternoon. The next morning, while all the other people were working, Jedidiah and Ayita checked out the new device. It was a large wheel with the tracing of a woman in the center, the arms and legs extended. There were six straps to place bottles in. The whole thing was mounted on edge and on an axle so that it could spin. Jedidiah mumbled, "Everyone sure has faith in me."

Ayita told him she trusted him completely and she was ready for anything he wanted to do. He looked at her wondering just what she meant by that.

Everything was loaded onto the train for the trip to Philadelphia. On the train ride, Jedidiah took his six gun apart to clean it and change a worn firing pin. Buffalo Bill came by while he was repairing it and watched for a short time. "Can I show you an easier way? Buffalo Bill asked. Jedidiah was happy for the help and learned quickly, Buffalo Bill helped him replace the firing pin. "The way you're shooting, and as fast as you're doing it, you might have to change that every few weeks," Buffalo Bill said. Jedidiah quickly learned to fix the gun and offered to work on his. This pleased Buffalo Bill. "We have several guns that might need repair from time to time. You should make a list of every gun the troop has, Jedidiah, and note the parts that might be needed to repair them. I can pick up the parts in Philadelphia."

Jedidiah talked to everyone using guns in the troop and made his list. Annie told him she thought that her rifle might need a new spring. He finished his list of weapons and the parts needed.

During the evening show, Jedidiah rode into the area to see Ayita spinning on the wheel. He galloped by and rapidly fired all six shots, busting the six bottles around Ayita. The crowd cheered and all came to their feet applauding. Cody smiled, knowing he had another hit. They performed Tuesday, Wednesday, Thursday, and Friday at six in the afternoon. Saturday, they performed at noon and again at seven. Sunday morning, they took everything down and loaded it onto the train. They were pushed with time loading the train as it needed to leave by five. It would take all night and all the next day and night to get to Philadelphia. That was their next stop, and they were to perform Tuesday through Saturday again there.

***

As soon as the tent was up and everyone was getting everything else ready, Buffalo Bill went into town. He bought the parts that Jedidiah needed along with books on every gun type. He had them all sent to the show. He then went to the newspaper office and picked up the flyers and spread them around town. Then he went to the telegraph office. He received some messages which he read, and sent out one to New York City and another to Boston. Those were their next stops according to his plan. He thought that if all went well, they might stay in New York for ten days. Buffalo Bill then went to the show and changed into his costume. He got saddled and led the parade through the streets of Philadelphia.

The parade wound its way around the town and back to the meadow where the show was set up. They immediately began selling tickets for the show. They had a packed house every night and Saturday at noon. Six performances, each with a cheering crowd.

Buffalo Bill checked the telegraph office early Saturday morning and had a telegraph from New York City. They would not need the tent. They had a large coliseum they could use, and it even had places for their livestock. The best part was it held over six times as many people as his tent could. They would get thirty percent of the gate and Buffalo Bill would get seventy. They would sell the tickets and settle with him each night after the show.

New York City went really well, and they had a packed house every night. Cody called the troop all together Saturday night after the show. He had collected from the gates and had more money than all the shows they had done so far put together. He paid the crew their share for the shows in New York already, even though they had four more shows to go. He told them to take tomorrow off other than caring for the stock and enjoy New York. To be at the show by eight Monday morning to prepare the evening show. Jedidiah asked Cody if he could be a little late Monday morning as he had some business, he would like to take care of. Cody told him it would be fine.

On Sunday morning, Jedidiah and Ayita walked the streets of New York City. Even though it was Sunday morning, there were a few businesses open. At noon, they found an enticing café facing the park. They sat at a table on the street and ordered their lunch. Later, they went to the edge of the island where they could look down the river and see the ocean. They both stood there with their mouths open in wonder. Jedidiah and Ayita were both amazed at the immensity of the city. Neither had ever imagined such a city or so many people. Some of the people were very different too, all different shades of skin color, and they had no idea where these people came from. Several times they heard people speaking in tongues they had never heard of before. Jedidiah even saw another dwarf like him. It was the first time he had seen another small person like himself. He had read about it in school but never seen it.

Ayita was taller than him, but even then, she was short for her people. She never said anything or acted like he was different or short. It was the first time they had really gotten away from the show together. Both had a really good time and enjoyed their day. That evening, they found a nice restaurant with a small band playing. Jedidiah ordered a bottle of wine with their meal, and they sat till late enjoying the evening together. He walked with her back to their hotel and to her door. She leaned down to him, and he kissed her, then said goodnight. It was Jedidiah's first kiss and Ayita's as well. Jedidiah went to his room and thought of that kiss for a long time.

By Monday morning, Jedidiah and Ayita met to eat breakfast together when Buffalo Bill Cody and Annie Oakley came in. They sat with them.

"What business do you have to attend to, Jedidiah?" Buffalo Bill asked.

"I need to deposit some of my money into the bank." Jedidiah didn't tell Buffalo Bill though that he was going to send some home and ask the sheriff to fix up his house. Ayita asked if she could go along as well; she could deposit some of her money and save it till it was needed. Buffalo Bill told them both that it was a grand idea, and they should do that. He then told them he was proud of them, for that was thinking ahead to their futures.

The other four shows went as well as the first and they were paid again after the last one in New York City. That last evening, Buffalo Bill Cody told them they were going to Boston next and after that, they would board a ship and go to London, England. The show would then tour Europe before returning here to New York City. They would play again here before deciding what to do after that. Anyone who doesn't want to go to Europe, I need to know between now and the show in Boston. I hope you all will continue with me though. We won't be using the tent in Boston, either, as the town has a large coliseum for us to use."

Chapter 12: On to Europe

The train ride to Boston took six and a half hours. During the ride, each crew member talked to Buffalo Bill Cody and told him they would be going on to Europe together. After they arrived in Boston, unloaded, and moved everything to the coliseum, Buffalo Bill told them that a group of Sioux were joining them for the show. For the act Sitting Bull would lead the Sioux to charge in from one direction, while Buffalo Bill would lead a group of white men dressed in Calvary uniforms and charge in from the other direction. They would be firing blanks with so many in such close proximity.

Annie Oakley said, "That sounds like a wild west show to me!" That received a laugh from everyone.

The train ride to Boston did not take long and they arrived with plenty of daylight to unload. Once unloaded, they moved everything to the coliseum. The tent, portable stock pens, and ticket booth had been put in storage in Philadelphia. Cody told them they could sleep late the next day, but to be at the coliseum by nine in the morning to set up. They all went to the hotel.

Jedidiah noticed the Sioux wore pants and western shirts but looked uncomfortable in them. Sitting Bull and Buffalo Bill said it would be better for them in these clothes around the city. They had brought their own clothes although Buffalo Bill had costumes for them. They all entered the hotel together and the manager greeted them with a smile. He told them that he was expecting them and had their rooms ready, per the telegram William Cody had sent. Buffalo Bill signed for all the rooms, and they picked up their keys. He had arranged for Annie and Ayita to share a room next to Jedidiah. Texas Jack shared a room with Jedidiah. Buffalo Bill enjoyed a suite to himself just down the hall.

The Buffalo Bill Cody Wild West Show played in Boston Tuesday through the second Thursday night, with two shows on Saturday. Again, the troop had Sunday off to enjoy the town. The ship that was to carry them to London, England, was at the loading dock. On Sunday, Buffalo Bill went to inspect the ship and talk to the captain. "We will pack our things Thursday night and bring them to the dock during the night."

"Good," the captain said. "I will have your things loaded on the ship early Friday morning and we will be ready to sail right after noon. She's an older ship; it will take eleven days to sail from Boston to London."

Jedidiah and Ayita walked around Boston that Sunday and found a café that was open. They talked about the ocean trip, wondering what it would be like. Ayita asked if Jedidiah knew anything about Europe and what to expect there. He told her all he knew were the things he had read in books. It seemed similar yet very different from the big cities here. He then added that other than England, many places have their own language. In Paris, they would be speaking French. In Spain, it would be Spanish, and so on. That was what he had read anyway. Ayita told him she had learned a little French from a woman from New Orleans. Jedidiah, himself, learned a little Spanish and Comanche. She laughed and told him she would help him learn some Cherokee.

Later, Jedidiah told Buffalo Bill he would work on all the guns on the trip across the Atlantic. "All the guns will be in top working condition when we start the shows," Jedidiah said. Cody agreed and told him that it would be a good idea. They finished the shows in Boston with a packed house each performance. Again, Buffalo Bill paid the troop… with extra money than expected. Friday morning before the ship sailed, Jedidiah, Ayita, and Buffalo Bill went to a bank and made deposits to their respective accounts. Buffalo Bill got a letter of credit to take with him in case he needed extra money in Europe. He had heard that in most cities they would be able to use a large building like the coliseum. He had also heard that they had large circuses there and more than one tent company making three ring tents.

Most of the gear was already loaded when Buffalo Bill, Annie, Jedidiah, and Ayita boarded the ship. Jedidiah found the room he was sharing with three other men, including Texas Jack.

"Did you have a good time with the little lady?" Jack asked.

Jedidiah smiled. "Yes." He stowed his things away then went on deck. He was anxious to get out on the ocean to see what it was like. He was standing at the rail when Ayita joined him. They were still standing there when the ship began to move. Slowly, they moved out of the harbor and into the Atlantic. A crewman walked by and told them they needed to go below to the galley as the meal was about to be served. It was dark by the time they finished eating and went back on deck. They couldn't see anything, so they separated and went back to their rooms.

After breakfast the first morning, Jedidiah went to the hold and checked on Goliath. He took along a sugar cube and gave it to his longtime friend. Once he was certain that Goliath was okay, he went back to his room. He began working on the guns belonging to the troop. Jedidiah took breaks only during mealtimes. During the meals, he sat with and talked to Ayita. He told her he would finish his work by noon the next day and they could spend some time together.

Hanska, one of the Sioux, came to Ayita while she stood alone at the rail on the forward deck. He asked her why she spent time with the little white man. He then told her she should have a warrior like him. She told him that Jedidiah was a good man, and she liked him. Hanska told her she would be his woman one day. Ayita walked away from him.

On the second day, Ayita and Jedidiah walked to the foredeck and watched the ocean. Ayita nudged Jedidiah and pointed to the six Sioux on the deck. "Look," she said, "the Sioux are amazed by the ocean." The Sioux stared at the water and looked around for land. "They did the same thing the day before."

Hanska was with the Sioux, and he glared at Jedidiah. Howahkan, the Sioux leader, told Hanska not to cause problems. They had promised Buffalo Bill Cody they would not cause problems. They were to be paid well and would use the money to buy many things their people needed.

It was a calm day, and the ship was making good time. The ship's crew did their best to make each of the troop comfortable. After the evening meal, Jedidiah and Ayita walked on the deck and looked at the moonlight upon the ocean. They began talking about the future and what each wanted in their future.

A few days later, an announcement came that they were in the Celtic Sea and would soon be able to see the coast of England. They would be passing into the English Channel, then rounding a bend into the Thames River.

Jedidiah and Ayita stood on the deck watching as the first sight of England came into view. "Is this truly another land on the other side of the world from home?" Ayita asked.

"Not the other side but part way around the world," Jedidiah said. "This is an island but not nearly as large as America." He then explained to her that the cities here were much larger and very old compared to New York and Boston. "The ways of the people here may be different, too," Jedidiah added.

An officer came to the rail near them and told them they were coming up on the point at Dungeness. He then explained that it wouldn't be long after that they would see the white cliffs of Dover. After they passed Dover, it was sometime later that the ship changed directions from northerly to westerly. They were moving towards the Thames River.

The ship docked at Chelsea Harbor as darkness fell across the city. The troop and their personal luggage were allowed to disembark. Everything else would be unloaded the next morning. Carriages were waiting to take them all to the hotel near the Earls Court. By the time they all arrived at their rooms, it was getting late in the evening. Many went together for dinner. Since most were there together, Buffalo Bill told them they would go early after breakfast to help move everything from the dock to the court. There were stables there for their livestock and a large field to set up in. Along one side, they would set teepees like an authentic Sioux village. Across the field they would set up western town front and a fort. There was a large, raised platform with permanent seating on top where dignitaries could sit. Around the field there was additional seating for all others. Altogether there were more seats than there had been in New York or Boston, he had been advised that even during the day, people would pay to walk through the town and village. Thursday they would have only a morning show at 9:30. This would be for Queen Victoria, members of parliament, Lords, Dukes, and Earls. The queen would come from the palace in a parade of her guards and royal entourage. They would wait to start the show till she was there and seated. They could expect to be delayed up to thirty minutes or more.

Buffalo Bill then asked Annie and Jedidiah to wait to see him after the meal. He told them that their targets would be placed so that they would be shooting in the opposant direction of the queen. He then told them that they were to be very careful not to turn her direction with a gun in their hands. If they were to turn, a sharpshooter of the Royal Guard would drop them in their tracks. This was all demanded by the Court. Jedidiah told him not to worry;

he would never point his gun at her. Buffalo Bill told them not to make the mistake of even giving them any doubt that they might shoot in that direction.

Hanska had been looking for an opportunity to challenge or do away with the little cowboy. He was getting more desperate each time he saw him with the Cherokee maiden, Ayita. During the first performance in London, Hanska saw his chance and seized it. In the course of the mock battle between Sioux and Calvary he shot his arrow at Jedidiah. They were supposed to hit the wagons and barrels placed before the troops. Jedidiah was on a platform behind a fake fort facade. The troops were firing blanks, which emitted a considerable amount of smoke. Just as Hanska fired his arrow, Jedidiah ducked below the facade to reload, having fired his single shot rifle. The arrow struck the backdrop behind the spot Jedidiah's chest would have been. Buffalo Bill and Sitting Bull both saw the attempt and Buffalo Bill had Jedidiah stay down below the fort wall lying on the platform till the mock battle was over. Sitting Bull moved closer to Hanska and told him to drop his bow and lay on the ground as if he were dead, or else he would be. All the crowd saw was a realistic reenactment of a western battle.

Sitting Bull and Howahkan kept Hanska far away from Jedidiah till the show was over that night. The Sioux tied Hanska up till late that night and the entire troop came together around him. Buffalo Bill Buffalo Bill, Sitting Bull, and Howahkan met together to discuss Hanska. Together they told the entire troop what happened. This disgraced Hanska and the Sioux. Jedidiah suggested that Hanska's weapons all be taken, and he would not be allowed to touch another gun, bow, tomahawk, or knife till he returned home. Buffalo Bill agreed and added that he was to clean the stables and conduct all the menial tasks around the show till they went home. He also told him that if he did anything else wrong, he would be left in jail in whatever country they were in. He might never see his home again. It was the duty of the Sioux to see to it that he stayed out of trouble and tended to his tasks. Buffalo Bill left it to them to police their own man.

The rest of the shows in London went without any trouble. There was a delay on Thursday of forty-five minutes. They waited until the queen arrived and was seated before the show started. The majority of the ministers and nobility were already there and waiting as well. Buffalo Bill Cody directed the show from his horse, making certain that it was the best performance they had put on. After the show an attendant to the queen came to Buffalo Bill and told him that Queen Victoria enjoyed the performance. He and five others of his choice were invited to dinner at the palace. A carriage would be picking them up at their hotel.

Buffalo Bill Cody selected Annie Oakley, Sitting Bull, Texas Jack, Ayita, and Jedidiah to accompany him to the palace for dinner. He suggested they go in costume without their weapons. He wore his frilly buckskin outfit and iconic western hat. Annie donned her buckskins and hat. Sitting Bull also wore his buckskins and full war bonnet. Jedidiah wore a black shirt and pants with a black hat. Over his shirt he wore a black leather vest. They were standing together in front of the hotel when the carriage pulled up to collect them. A man stepped off the rear of the carriage to open the door for them. A gentleman rode inside with them and explained the protocol to them. By the time they arrived at the palace, they were well versed in what they should and should not do.

The dinner went well with the queen asking questions of each of them and making pointed remarks. For Jedidiah, she asked him how he came to ride such a massive horse. He told her that Goliath was the first horse he met, and they had become friends. She told him that at first, she believed him to be a court jester, but she quickly learned that he was a western knight riding his charger. At this, Ayita touched his arm and smiled at him. After dinner, they were taken back to the hotel in the carriage. The next day, they prepared for another show. They performed for two weeks in London.

On their day off, Jedidiah and Ayita walked around to see the sights of London. Just outside of the Earl's Court, they found a street merchant selling pictures. He had pictures of all the sights in London, but also of the Buffalo Bill Cody Wild West Show. He agreed to take a picture of them together and placed them on the platform where the queen had sat. He said he would have it ready for them the next day. They found a trolley and the driver was friendly and told them which stops to take for the best scenery. They enjoyed their day and found a café to eat at before returning to the hotel.

The rest of the shows in London went without any other problems. After the last show, they began preparing everything to take back to the ship. It would be waiting for them at the same dock. Once they were all loaded, the ship would ease back down the Thames and into the channel before going up the Seine to Paris. Buffalo Bill had sent a letter, and they were expected in Paris for two weeks. Jedidiah and Ayita had seen very little of Hanska, which did not bother either of them. By the end of the next day, everything was loaded onto the ship. Everyone had their things in the rooms and stood together at the rail on the ship's deck. The ship slowly pulled away from the dock. Minutes later, they were slowly moving down the river towards open water. By the time the ship reached open water, it was dark, and the city lights sparkled. Being time for dinner, they went in to eat and sat together. It was to take five days aboard the ship before they docked in Paris. Most of the time would be on the channel and navigating the Seine. Paris, they were told, was over one hundred miles from the coast but twice the distance by following the river to get there.

Chapter 13: Train Across Europe

Five days after leaving London, they docked in Paris, France. The next several hours were much the same as every other day of arrival. In Paris though, everything was inspected as it was unloaded and before they were allowed to move from the port. There were wagons and plenty of help to move everything from the port to Cirque d'Hiver Bouglion where they were to perform. It was a large indoor venue with the largest seating capacity they've experienced. The price of tickets would be higher than Buffalo Bill had anticipated but so would each of their take.

At Cirque d'Hiver, there was an entrance to the left of the main doors for them to unload the wagons and livestock. There were stables at the ground level of a multi-floored attached building behind the round coliseum. There were rooms for the entire troop in the building on the second and third floors. Buffalo Bill arranged for Annie, Jedidiah, Ayita, and himself to stay at a hotel down the street. This pleased Jedidiah and Ayita. Not only could they see each other more often, but it might keep them out of sight of Hanska. They would be performing every day for two weeks and twice on Saturdays. Their Sunday performances would be late in the afternoon. The only time they would get off would be a few hours here and there in the early hours of the day.

They learned that President Marie Joseph Louis Adolphe Thiers would attend the Sunday afternoon performance. His personal guard would be around him, and many local dignitaries would be there that day also. The shows were going well, and Jedidiah and Ayita managed to get away one morning. The couple went to the arts district. They tried the local coffee with croissants. Ayita stopped in front of an artesian working on a pottery wheel. She told Jedidiah she had learned to make pottery as a child. The way they worked was different, but their work was beautiful. She talked to the artisan for some time about techniques. Jedidiah watched and smiled at the joy she was getting from conversing about pottery. All too soon, they had to return to the Cirque to prepare for the show.

On another day out they once again found a photographer who had taken pictures of the show. They bought pictures of the Cirque with the wild west show and some of the city of Paris. These were light and took up little space. They would be able to keep the pictures as a reminder of this time together in Europe. For two weeks the show went successfully. Jedidiah and Ayita went through the streets of Paris on the mornings they were able to. On Sunday evening after the show, they managed to get away and ate at a café below the arts district. After eating, they went across the avenue into the Le' Bar Masc. They shared a bottle of wine with a picture of Shakespeare on it before returning to the hotel.

Hanska no longer cared about what happened to himself, having been humiliated by the little white man. The maid would be his, or he would die trying. There was no chance of getting a weapon, but he was certain that he would be able to kill the little white one with his bare hands. He worked late on Sunday, knowing that they would be out walking around the city. After leaving the Cirque Hanska walked into the dark street. He stayed in the shadows as he approached the entrance to the hotel Jedidiah and Ayita were staying. Knowing that neither of them would be armed as it was not allowed in this city, he positioned himself and waited for them to appear. Once he heard laughter and saw them coming along a side street toward him. The sound of a slight movement made him look back as four of the Sioux jumped him.

The four Sioux tied Hanska's hands behind his back and carried him to the coliseum. Howahkan, the Sioux Chief, informed Buffalo Bill Cody, who sent for Sitting Bull, as he wanted both Howahkan and Sitting Bull's agreement on what had to be done. After the meeting, Hanska was kept tied up in a stable for the rest of the night. The next morning, the Paris police were summoned. After hearing the story, they informed Buffalo Bill, Sitting Bull, and Howahkan that if they filed such a charge, he would be tried. If he were found guilty of trying to kill Jedidiah, he would face the guillotine. Buffalo Bill explained that to Sitting Bull, who nodded his head and confirmed that the warrior had been warned and made his decision. If he had done his work and stayed out of trouble till they went home, all would have been forgotten. Hanska was turned

over to the Paris police and none of them ever saw him
again.

Buffalo Bill told Jedidiah and Ayita what had
happened, and they both shook their heads. Once Ayita was
told what would happen to Hanska she gasped. She told
Jedidiah that would be one of the worst ways for an Indian
to die. They believed that a headless corpse could not find
their way to the happy hunting grounds. He would wander
in the "Between Place" forever.

The Wild West Show finished the shows in Paris.
They loaded everything onto an awaiting train. This train
stayed with them till Rome. From Paris, though, the
itinerary was to go to Brussels, Belgium. After a short ride,
they unloaded the train bringing the day to an end. They
would be staying only five days in Brussels and performing
in another indoor arena.

They were soon unloading the train and moving into
the arena. Once everything was moved into the coliseum
and the stock fed and bedded down, they settled into their
hotel nearby for the next five evening performances. Then
it would be back onto the train. After the first performance
they were asked to add an extra performance on the third
day an hour before noon. This performance was for the
royal house and their guests. They would be paid for a
packed house.

The shows went as expected with a packed house
each performance. At the end, each member was paid well
for their contributions.

Jedidiah and Ayita found one morning they were able
to get away for a few hours to visit the city. They were both
amazed at the museums and churches in Europe. They were

also pleasantly surprised at the acceptance of them as a couple. Other than Hanska, Jedidiah had not been tormented by anyone on the trip. The Europeans all acknowledged him as an equal. Many in Brussels spoke French and another language that they did not recognize. Fortunately, there was usually someone nearby that could speak English.

At one place, though, the locals refused to speak English so that the couple could understand. Ayita became annoyed and started speaking to them in Cherokee. They stopped speaking and looked at her in awe and asked in English, "What is that language?"

Laughing, she said, "Cherokee, my native tongue."

Jedidiah then spoke in Comanche. They said that it sounded different. He told them that it was Commanche, another Indian tribe. After that, those people spoke English around them. They found another photographer and bought pictures of many things of interest to them. The five days were soon over, and they were on a train leaving Belgium.

The next city to perform at was Amsterdam. Once the train was unloaded, they took their gear and stock to the Koninklijk Theater Carre. It was a coliseum in the city. Here, they all needed interpreters. A few did speak English and helped them. They only stayed for four performances. When Jedidiah and Ayita went out to see the city, they were surprised to see Amsterdam was on a large bay with many canals instead of streets. They were able to get a ride on a small boat that gave them a tour along the canals. It was so different from anything either of them had ever seen.

After four days of shows, they were loading up

again on the train. Jedidiah and Ayita had again bought some pictures of the city and the building the show was in. They were excited about the next part of their journey, for they would have six days on the train before they reached their next destination. They would have many short stops to refuel and allow other trains to pass. At some of these stops, they would be allowed to leave the train for a short time. Their next show would be in Berlin, Germany. They had to take the long way around to go through Belgium and Deutschland due to the recent conflict between France and Germany. Though not at war at the time, direct border crossings were not allowed.

The first day's stop was in a town where no one could pronounce the name, nor did it look familiar. They stayed on the train eating and sleeping there. The second day, they came to Hamburg, Germany. Many were ready to get off for the two-hour delay they would have. Jedidiah and Ayita walked a short distance to find a place to eat. As they entered, they saw Buffalo Bill, Annie, and Sitting Bull at a table. They sat next to them and enjoyed a rich German meal. Jedidiah tried the dark beer and was surprised how much he liked it. After eating, they all got back onto the train, and it shortly began moving again. They had one shorter stop along the way. The train pulled into the station and stopped in Berlin by noon. They quickly unloaded onto the dock. The authorities there checked everything as items were unloaded.

Everything was taken to the Markthallen Circus. It was a large building used specifically for the circus. It could hold up to forty-five hundred people and would be the perfect site for the Wild West Show. Again, the language was a bit of a problem, but they had learned to deal with that. Once everything was inside, they checked into a hotel nearby. The hotel had been prearranged and was expecting them. The entire troop was in the same hotel and no one else was staying there. Buffalo Bill Cody had arranged for morning meals in the dining hall for the entire crew.

At breakfast the first morning he told them all they were about as far away from home as they would get on this trip. He told them they would start work right after breakfast preparing the show. Once more they would get Sundays off but would be performing for ten days here. After leaving Berlin they would be going to Prague. That was as far east as they would go. He thanked them and promised to continue paying them bonuses to match the crowds that attended. The shows all went off without any problems. Each performance had a sold-out crowd. On Sunday many went out to see the city. Jedidiah and Ayita went together. The city was different yet similar to the others they had visited. The food was good, and Jedidiah really liked the beer.

One evening, the show was delayed, and everyone stood waiting. When the emperor arrived and took a seat, everyone sat, and the show started. Each show performed to a packed house, and on the last night, Buffalo Bill Cody paid all the troops their pay with bonuses. All of the members were happy with the amount of money they were making. The next morning, they packed everything up and loaded it all on the train. Fortunately, this leg of the trip would only take one day as the train would be traveling at top speed with no stops along the way. It was still daylight when they pulled into Prague. Everyone agreed the view of the city was amazing when they looked out the windows. Although they were far from the ocean, Jedidiah saw large ocean-going ships as they crossed the river. They passed ports along the river and were able to see that Prague was an old and large city. They looked forward to performing in the city's Myers Circus.

The troop was to perform in Prague for ten days. Buffalo Bill Cody promised they'd have Sunday off again. After everything was moved from the train station and stored away with Myers Circus, everyone checked into the hotel before dark. Many ate with Buffalo Bill at the hotel. Jedidiah and Ayita went and found a café nearby. The food was similar to German food, but the sauerkraut was not as strong. Jedidiah did not like the beer; it seemed bitter to him.

As they walked back to the hotel holding hands, Ayita wondered if Jedidiah would ever ask her to be his woman. It had been long enough, and she thought he should be making offers for her to Buffalo Bill. She knew that he understood some of the Indian ways, but perhaps he did not know hers.

At the door to her room, she asked him if he wanted her. He told her yes, but he figured he would have to wait to speak with her father. She told him that would be proper, and he would have to offer him a good horse and a good gun, or perhaps many horses. Jedidiah told her that was what he thought and that he would have to wait till he could present such an offer to her father. He said goodnight to her and left to go to his room. Ayita was happy as she went to bed that night. She could and would wait as long as it took.

She knew he was a good man; he would be good to her and make her happy.

After loading onto the train in Prague, they went to Vienna. It was a seven-hour trip on the train. They were able to unload but left everything on the docks overnight. The stock was kept in pens and cared for at the train station. The next morning, everything was moved to The Rotunda. The world's fair had been there and now it was time for the Buffalo Bills Wild West Show. They would stay a week and large crowds were expected. The center held many more people than any place they had been. The tickets would not be overly expensive but that would help pack the house. Buffalo Bill expected to make more money at this venue than before.

East Europe did not disappoint them; the people came from miles around to see the wild west show from America. None had seen American Indians before or a buffalo. Sitting Bull, Buffalo Bill Cody, Annie Oakley, Texas Jack, and Jedidiah were all big hits. At the end of their time in Vienna, they loaded on the train. Jedidiah and Ayita had spent a few hours alone in the city but had not spoken of their love or of becoming joined. Jedidiah knew very little of such things but knew he wanted to spend the rest of his life with Ayita. He planned on going all the way to Oklahoma to speak to her father and give him all he had if needed for her. He was sure that she wanted him, and he wanted to do what was right. He just was not sure what that was.

The train left Vienna and seven hours later they had a stopover in Venice, Italy. Jedidiah and Ayita left the train for an hour to see the city. They could not believe that the entire city floated on a lagoon along the sea. They had never dreamed of such. Ayita could not believe the ingenuity of the white man. They had a good meal of fish together then returned to the train. They rode the train all night and arrived in Rome, Italy around noon. Both had heard of Rome and were eager to see the ancient city. They were both hoping they would have plenty of opportunities to see the sights of this intriguing floating city.

The Buffalo Bill Cody Wild West Show unloaded from the train in Rome. They moved everything from the train station to the coliseum where they were to perform. They would be here for two weeks. A day before they were to leave, their ship would join them here and be docked, waiting for them to load. Buffalo Bill Cody promised the entire troop they would have both Sundays off and would be able to see everything they wanted to in Rome. The first show was a hit and word spread throughout the region about the great western show. Many people came.

Jedidiah and Ayita went into the city to see the sights. They found a nice café to eat, and Jedidiah asked her, "How should I go about talking to your father back in Oklahoma?"

Ayita dropped her fork and stared at him. She finally answered, "Bill Cody traded an exceptionally good horse and a repeating rifle for me. My father told him I was his woman. He told my father that he would be my father, but not my man. Bill Cody is the one you would need to talk to and trade for me."

With a sigh of relief, Jedidiah told her he would do that as soon as he could get Buffalo Bill alone.

Early the next morning Jedidiah got Buffalo Bill Cody alone in the lobby of the hotel. He declared his love for Ayita Buffalo Bill wondered what took him so long to get around to marrying the girl. Jedidiah told him he thought he would have to wait till they got to Oklahoma. Buffalo Bill gave Jedidiah his permission and said he would not take a horse or a gun. "It would probably be simpler if you all married on the ship in international waters," Buffalo Bill said.

Jedidiah talked to Ayita, and they agreed to wait till they were on the ship and get married between Rome and Barcelona, Spain. The ship was supposed to meet them in Rome a day before they left.

Every show went by slowly to Jedidiah, but they were a success. At the end, they all received a large bonus, but not as much as Jedidiah and Ayita, the girl that had become like a daughter to him was given more. Buffalo Bill Cody searched Rome to find as many white buckskins as he could. He took them to the native women in the troop, telling them about the pending marriage so that they could make a special Cherokee bridal dress. The dress was made from a white buckskin and instead of glass beads, they adorned it with precious jewels, diamonds, emeralds, and rubies. All this was done without Jedidiah's or Ayita's knowledge. Although Rome was a beautiful city, everyone was eager to leave. Every member of the troop knew of Jedidiah and Ayita's love for one another and approved of it. All got to see Rome and many of its historic sights. They all eagerly boarded the ship, ready to sail. The first thing Buffalo Bill Cody did was to talk to the ship's captain. They decided on the second day around midmorning for the wedding. The captain, being well aware of Jedidiah and Ayita's feelings for each other, was happy to be a part of their life together.

Ayita had been given the best cabin on the ship, Buffalo Bill's. She had the cabin all alone too. Jedidiah was in a cabin next to her. They were kept apart by every one of the troop. They were allowed to dine together but sat at a table with Buffalo Bill and Annie. It had been decided that Buffalo Bill would walk Ayita down the aisle as her father. Sitting Bull would be Jedidiah's best man and Annie Oakley would be Ayita's maid of honor.

Before dawn of the second morning, they passed through the straight between Corsica and Sardinia. By noon, they were well into international waters, which gave the captain full authority to marry a couple. The captain, Jedidiah, and Sitting Bull stood in front of the troop. The big event was held in the dining hall of the ship. Everyone was able to be there. Buffalo Bill Cody and Ayita walked down the aisle. She wore a white buckskin dress with frilly leather streamers down each arm and legs. Lined all along the dress were precious stones glittering in white, green, and red. On her head was a jewel-crusted Tiera that Buffalo Bill bought for her, saying she was a princess. She was easily the most beautiful woman on the ship. She approached Jedidiah, who was dressed in a suit with long tails and a tie. He felt nobody could be more uncomfortable than him. One look at Ayita coming down the aisle toward him relieved all his anxiety.

After the ceremony they were served a meal with the couple sitting in front of everyone. Annie Oakley brought up a package and handed it to Ayita. "The crew all chipped in and got this for you," Annie said.

Ayita opened it to find a complete pottery set with tools and a wheel. Texas Jack came up with a package for Jedidiah. It was a complete tool set for gunsmiths. By sunset, they arrived at Barcelona.

The newlywed couple was checked into the best room at the hotel. Buffalo Bill had talked to them and asked them to perform the three nights they would be in Barcelona. He didn't ask them to help set up or take care of any of the chores around the show. Everyone else helped unload the ship and cared for the stock. Buffalo Bill told Jedidiah not to worry about Goliath; he would personally get the horse off the ship and take care of him. Buffalo Bill had another surprise for them.

The show was performed for three days in Barcelona. Jedidiah and Ayita should have their bags packed before the last show started. As soon as it was over, they were to board the ship. The ship would be cleaned and loaded with cargo by then. Buffalo Bill told them they were to take a few days off and steam with the ship. It was going to Casablanca to unload its cargo then steam to Lisbon Portugal. The show would travel by train to Madrid, spend a week performing there, then meet the couple in Lisbon.

Jedidiah and Ayita went aboard the ship and were shown to the best cabin. It was the cabin that Bill Cody had been using. The captain invited them to dine with him that night after telling them they would sail within the hour.

Chapter 14: The Return

Not long after they felt the ship move, Jedidiah heard the whistle announcing dinner. Ayita and Jedidiah dressed in their best for the captain and strolled hand in hand to the dining hall. Over dinner, the captain advised them to be on deck shortly after breakfast. They would be passing through the Strait of Gibraltar. It would be a sight worth seeing. "We will pass within view of the Rock of Gibraltar and should be able to see both continents as we go through the straight," the captain said. He then told them that by the end of the following day, they would be docked in Casablanca.

The captain then explained to them that before they arrived at Casablanca they may run into some problems. There had been reports of pirates operating in the area. "If we spot a pirate and they move toward us, I will get word to you. You may want to arm yourself. I understand that you are an excellent shot."

Jedidiah told him he had a handgun and rifle. He then explained that he also had his Sharps fifty that Buffalo Bill gave him. "I can hit a fly at four hundred yards," Jedidiah stated.

Ayita and Jedidiah watched from the deck as they passed the Rock of Gibraltar. They stood on the bow of the ship and soon were able to see land on either side of them.

To the right was Europe and to the left was Africa. They were on their way to visit Africa. They would only see one city though and it was in the desert, not the jungles. The captain had also told them there was slave trading going on in the area, and the British were trying to stop it. Casablanca was not under British rule; it was governed by France. After they left sight of the coast, Jedidiah and Ayita went to their cabin. An hour later, the ship's bell rang. Jedidiah strapped his pistol on his side and put on a jacket, filling the pockets with ammunition. He grabbed his Henry rifle in one hand and his Sharps in the other and ran onto the deck. Ayita brought as much ammunition as she could find and followed him. They went to the upper deck by the bridge.

A crewman told them the captain said a pirate ship was approaching fast. If they came within range, he was free to fire on them. The crewman then added that he shouldn't hold back his fire. If the pirates take them, it wouldn't be nice what they would do to the lady, before they sold her into slavery.

The captain was on the bridge watching the pirate ship when a crew member told him there was another ship coming from the opposite direction. Looking through his glass, he quickly identified the new ship as a British war ship. Help was on the way. The captain then told the helmsman to turn directly toward the British ship. They would close the distance between them. He also told the helmsman not to get directly between them as they may open fire with their cannons. They heard a rumble and looked back at the British ship to see smoke from the bow.

It had fired its forward eight-inch guns. The captain then heard a single boom from his ship.

He stepped out on the deck to see Jedidiah reloading his sharps. "Are you close enough?" the captain asked.

Jedidiah told him, "I just dropped someone who was looking through a glass at us on the pirate ship's bridge. I missed the glass but took off most of his head." He shot again and hit another pirate. Ayita told him to let her reload the Sharps and handed him the Henry rifle. Jedidiah raised the sights and fired it. Levering another round into the chamber, he sighed down the barrel and shot again. With every shot, a pirate dropped, not to get up again. By now, whoever was in charge on that ship turned it around. They knew a British war ship was closing and there was a shooter on the cargo vessel.

The British ship came alongside, asking if they needed assistance. The ship was the HMS Rattlesnake, a seventeen-gun corvette. They had witnessed the shooting from the cargo ship and asked about it. The captain told them that an American from the Buffalo Bill Cody Wild West Show was on board and had fired back at the pirates.

Commodore John Edmund Commerell, who was in command of the British ship, said, "He must be some shooter as every shot we heard we saw a pirate drop dead."

The captain told him Jedidiah was a sharpshooter with the show. "He just got married. He and his wife are traveling with us."

They separated and went on to Casablanca. They docked well before dark. The captain told Jedidiah that Buffalo Bill had sent a message ahead and their hotel was already booked and paid for. He then told them they would have three nights here before leaving for Lisbon. The cargo would be unloaded and his new cargo loaded by then. He advised them, "If you go into the city, hire a guide at the hotel. You will be safer that way and the guide can take you to see the sights, or wherever you wish."

The crew carried their bags and insisted on the two of them walking ahead to the hotel; they'd follow behind with the luggage. Jedidiah told Ayita, "Now this is service."

The captain had told Jedidiah it would not only be allowed but advisable for him to carry his pistol here. They walked into the hotel and to the desk. Jedidiah asked if they spoke English. With a French accent, the man told him yes. Jedidiah told him they were supposed to have a reservation for him and his wife made by Bill Cody. The man told him they did, and it was the best room in the house. It was ready and waiting for them. He offered to show them to their room himself, and he had a porter carry their luggage. The man picked up a towel and bottle of champagne and guided them to their room. It took up all of one end of the top floor. He told them anything they needed; they only had to pull the rope hanging from the ceiling. It would ring a bell at the desk, and he would send someone to help them.

After the clerk and porter left, Jedidiah and Ayita looked around the rooms. There was a bedroom, a sitting room, and a washroom. Doors opened from both the sitting room and the bedroom to the outside. They opened one of them to find a balcony with sitting space and a view looking out over the ocean. Jedidiah asked Ayita if she would like to eat in the room tonight and she thought it was a lovely idea. He pulled the rope and waited while looking around. A few minutes later, they heard a tap at the door. He opened it to see the porter. He asked about having a meal brought to their room. The porter produced two menus from his inside coat pocket. Jedidiah thought that was insightful. Some of the dishes they had to ask the porter about but finally settled on what they wanted to eat. They had both selected something different as they had been trying new foods from the cities they visited.

Their meal was enjoyable except for a small bowl of steamed tiny balls that were bland, which neither of them liked. They didn't know what it was, but they did not like the taste. Jedidiah and Ayita went downstairs the next morning and asked the clerk about a guide. The clerk asked where they wanted to go and what they wanted to see. They told him one thing they wanted was to buy pictures of the city and places of worship. They would really like a picture of them in front of something recognizable to where they were at. They would also like to go shopping. The clerk smiled and said he would have the perfect person for them after they finished their breakfast.

Their guide spoke English very well and was knowledgeable of the city. He took them to the square where they found a photographer. He took a picture of them in the square with horses and camels in the background. He told them he would deliver it to their hotel by tomorrow morning. They bought several other pictures, many with African animals. They found a place that served coffee. They tried it and were surprised at how good it was. Somewhat different but good.

On their last night in Casablanca, they sat together on the balcony and watched the sun set on the water. Jedidiah reached over and held her hand. She looked at him and smiled. They knew they had to leave first thing in the morning, so they went back inside and packed most of their things. He had already told the clerk what time he wanted the porter at his door to bring their luggage down. At the specified time, the porter tapped at the door, and they were ready. They walked together down to the lobby and two crewmen from the ship were there waiting for them. A short time later, they were in their cabin on the ship, and it was building up steam to sail.

The sun was just coming up as the ship left the dock at Casablanca. It was a thirteen-hour cruise to Lisbon. The captain was trying to get there before dark. It was an old port and often very busy. He kept all the crew watching for the pirates, but they slipped by without running into them again. The trip to Lisbon was uneventful and the captain invited the newlywed couple to his table for lunch. He would be busy at dinner time, and they may wish to eat in Lisbon.

Jedidiah and Ayita had everything packed and ready to go as they went through the pass to Lisbon port. They were standing on the deck and watching as the ship slowly entered the port. As they passed through the mouth of the river into the narrow area, they saw a fort standing three stories tall with cannons at each level pointed at the river. Jedidiah pitied any ship trying to get past it. A short distance further, the river widened. The ship eased to the left to the port and docked. They were in Lisbon, Portugal, and their holiday was almost over. Buffalo Bill and the troop should arrive tomorrow, and they would have to get ready for the show.

Jedidiah and Ayita arrived at the hotel and found that once again, Buffalo Bill arranged a large, elegant room for them. On their way to the hotel, they spotted a nice little café with tables and chairs on the street under some trees. He asked her if she would like to come back there for dinner. A lady came to their table as soon as they sat down. They had a language problem till the lady went inside and a different lady came out. She spoke English and explained the menu for them. After dinner they could hear music coming from a basement door across the street. They saw people going in and out. Ayita asked the lady who served them what was happening and was told it was a bar with musicians playing. Holding hands, they walked across the street and entered the bar.

They found a table in the back corner and sat down. The people were very friendly and helpful. A man at the next table spoke English and helped them place an order then explained the music to them. They stayed for two hours before returning to their hotel.

The next morning, they walked around Lisbon, toured an old church, and shopped along the wide streets. Just after noon the members of the Buffalo Bill Cody Wild West Show arrived in Lisbon. Jedidiah and Ayita met them at the train station. Jedidiah went straight to check on Goliath. The giant horse nuzzled him as he gave him a carrot and a sugar cube. He led Goliath down the ramp off the train and to the pens at the coliseum while walking hand in hand with Ayita. Everyone worked hard unloading the train and moving everything to the coliseum.

Everything was prepared for them to perform in Lisbon for a week.

Each morning, Jedidiah and Ayita went to the pens so Jedidiah could feed and water Goliath. Goliath would greet them each time by pawing at the floor of the stall and raising his head up and down. Jedidiah smiled knowing that Goliath was happy to see him. After taking care of Goliath, the couple would venture out into the city. For them, it was an ancient and wondrous metropolis. The old chapels with antiquated beings hanging from its roof seem peculiar. Large statues of men on horseback with drawn swords in the middle of an intersection seemed odd. Each street that they went down though was a myriad of sights, sounds, smells, and tastes to be tried. Many of the foods they tried pleased them.

Knowing this was possibly their last days in Europe, Jedidiah and Ayita were eager to make the best of their time. Every free moment was spent together walking through the streets of Lisbon. They quickly learned that all the best of Europe was available here in Lisbon. They bought many items that interested them, including again photographs of the show and of the local city. Each show was going well, and they were fast approaching the time to board the ship for America.

After the last day of the show, they began packing everything to load on the ship. Though they had thoroughly enjoyed traveling through Europe and the short excursion to Africa, Jedidiah and Ayita were happy to be going back. The couple had been discussing where they would go to live. He described Santa Fe and she told him it sounded beautiful. Ayita asked if they could go through northeastern Oklahoma to see her family. He wholeheartedly agreed.

At the end of their last day in Europe, Buffalo Bill Cody paid them their share of the gate proceeds. It was much more than any of them were expecting.

Chapter 15: Going Home

Jedidiah and Ayita boarded the ship to New York from Lisbon and found they had a large cabin again. Jedidiah went to the hold and checked on Goliath twice each day. It was to be a twelve-and-a-half-day voyage back to New York City. On the first night aboard the steamship, Buffalo Bill called a meeting with the troop. He told them that he had received a letter in Lisbon asking for the show to be performed again in New York City. He told them that he would increase their share of the ticket sales if they stayed with him for a five-day show. Once it was over, they could each go their own way. They all agreed to stay with the show for the extra five days.

For dinner that first night they were again invited to the captain's table along with Buffalo Bill Cody and Annie Oakley. Ayita thought that it was a wonderful dinner and the food was excellent. She had learned the white man's way of formal dining and appreciated it. She appreciated how in formal settings they often treated her as a princess. Yes, her father was a minor chief, and amongst her people, she was considered a princess. However, she had learned about European royalty which seemed much more distinguished. To her, the title meant a lot more. She loved Jedidiah with all her heart. She had chosen him, but just as important, he had chosen her. She knew that he loved her dearly as he told her every day. Here she was sitting at a table with people who were well known anywhere in the world.

Jedidiah looked at his wife and noticed a distant look on her face. He whispered, "Is anything wrong?"

"No," Ayita answered. "I was just thinking about where I came from compared to where I am now. From teepees and buckskin to the captain's table and dining in royal palaces… it has been a large change."

"You are royalty and will always be to me," Jedidiah said.

"That is why I love you so much and always will," Ayita said.

On the ninth day of the voyage, they all awoke to the ship bouncing around. Many went to the dining hall where others gathered for information. Being breakfast time, they were all served a light repast of biscuits and coffee. Many were having trouble with their stomachs and did not wish to eat. It was sometime later before the second officer came into the dining hall and spoke to them. He informed them that they had come into a massive tropical storm and may have to turn south to avoid it. The storm was moving northwest the same as them and if they continued, they would quickly be in the center of the storm. Heading south would add days onto their journey but would be much safer for them all.

The ship turned south to avoid the hurricane before them. They went east of Bermuda then turned southwest. They followed behind the high winds of the hurricane as they traveled slowly west toward the coast of America. On the twelfth day, they made port in Norfolk, Virginia. The captain was not even certain of where they were until he spotted the coast. By that time, they were so low on fuel, they had to find a port. Happy to be in a friendly port, they paused long enough to refuel and take on necessary supplies. The ship and the Wild West Show was only a day's sail to New York City. Buffalo Bill left the ship to send a telegraph to New York to advise them they were a couple days off their time but would arrive the next day. He also talked to the authorities and learned that the hurricane had weakened, then moved north and east back out to sea. Once refueled, they would be able to leave and stay behind the bad weather and rough seas.

***

The Wild West Show made it to New York and unloaded. Buffalo Bill Cody and the troop all thanked the captain and wished him well. They moved everything to the coliseum and prepared for a show the next day. Since they had missed the planned first day, they would perform five shows in four days. They would do two shows on the last day.

Jedidiah and Ayita had a large room at the hotel near the coliseum. They ate breakfast at the hotel then walked together to the train station. They booked two tickets to Kansas along with a car for Goliath. They then walked around shopping for a few minutes before going to the coliseum to work and prepare for the show. Each morning, they bought things they believed they would need in Santa Fe. They also planned for the money which they had deposited there, to be sent to the bank in Santa Fe. After the last show, Buffalo Bill Cody paid each of them their wages plus a large bonus. He thanked them and told each of them if he started the show back up, he would be in touch with them. Jedidiah and Ayita, both told him no thanks.

At eleven the next morning, Jedidiah and Ayita were on a train going west from New York. They had several stops before they got off in Kansas City four days later. It was a little before dark when they stepped off the train hand in hand. Jedidiah helped unload Goliath and collected their things. He paid to have all their belongings taken to the hotel down the street. He placed Goliath in the livery stable for the night and asked the owner about buying a good pack mule.

Jedidiah and Ayita went to the hotel after taking care of Goliath. Once they were checked into their room, they went out to eat and discuss their next move. Jedidiah told her about his house in Missouri and that he intended to sell it. He will telegraph the sheriff tomorrow asking him to sell all his belongings there and to send all the money to the bank in Santa Fe. This would save him needing to go back there. He then suggested that they ride south from here to see her family in Oklahoma. She had talked about them, and he knew she missed them. They could get packs to transport all their belongings on the mule he just bought. The two of them could easily ride Goliath.

They stayed one more night in Kansas City before starting the long ride to Ayita's family's home. Jedidiah wanted them to know where she would be and that he would take good care of her. Early the second morning in Kansas City, the two rode out of the city on Goliath, with the mule trailing behind. Ayita knew where they were going, and they figured it would take nine days to get there. They shouldn't be passing any dangerous territory, but there was always the chance of running into outlaws.

Afternoon came and they were riding alongside a fair-sized creek. Jedidiah spotted a turkey and shot it. Ayita plucked the bird while they were riding and started laughing.

He asked her, "What are you laughing about?"

She told him, "I was thinking about plucking this bird after having sat at the queen's table."

They had a rope tied to the mule which followed behind with their belongings. Before dark they came to a fork in the creek where another smaller creek joined this one coming from the northwest. They crossed the smaller creek and found a nice campsite in some trees overlooking the fork. As Jedidiah cared for Goliath and the mule, Ayita gathered wood for a fire. Jedidiah put the saddle on the ground and smiled at Ayita.

"It's nice to have such lovely help making camp," Jedidiah said.

She smiled back at him. By the time he carried some water up from the creek, she had a fire going and the turkey cooking over the fire. Sitting around the fading fire, watching the heat dance over the red coals, they talked about their future. Ayita was excited about going to Santa Fe. Jedidiah explained about the trail there and that for many miles, water would be hard to find if not nonexistent. He also explained that it was a rough country between here and there, with many outlaws and dangerous Indians. "There are the Kiowa, Comanche, and Apache, among others. Best I can figure, it would be as much riding going straight from your family's place across Oklahoma and the Texas panhandle as it would to go back to Kansas City then ride the train to Dodge City. If we ride the train to Dodge City, we will still have to angle across the bad lands and across the Texas panhandle. It would be as much time on the trail by horseback either way. If we go across the territory, we will have water for more of the distance."

Ayita told him, "My father talked with many from the other tribes, and he might know if going across the Indian Territory would be best."

They rode together for five more days. Late in the afternoon on the sixth day after leaving Kansas City, Ayita squeezed Jedidiah's left arm. He looked around to see her nodding behind and to their left. Along a hill rode three Indian warriors. She told him it should be okay if they were Cherrokee. As evening came, they arrived at a river. Jedidiah led them across the river and began setting up camp. The warriors quietly rode near as Jedidah and Ayita got off Goliath. The warriors hadn't touched their weapons, so Jedidiah told Ayita to invite them into camp. She spoke to them in Cherokee, but one of them told her they spoke English. Jedidiah told him that they had food and would be happy to share their meal. The three rode into the camp and tied up their horses near Goliath. They stood near Goliath and held their hands to their heads comparing the height against the giant horse's side. With a puzzled look on their faces, they came to the fire and squatted down.

"Big horse," one of them said. He then looked at Ayita and spoke to her in Cherokee.

Ayita answered back in her native language before explaining to Jedidiah. "He wants to know who my people are. He knows about them. They will ride with us the rest of the way to my family."

During the next three days, their ride took them through many mountains with beautiful valleys. Many of the valleys had rivers and streams flowing through them with an abundance of game. On the afternoon of the third day, they arrived at the village where Ayita's family lived. Ayita said to her parents, "we traveled across the ocean to Europe and many great cities there."

Jedidiah spoke, "we plan on starting a business that Ayita will make pottery for and I will fix guns. We wish to start this shop in Santa Fe together.

Ayita's father asked, "why did you go so far out of your way to get here?"

Jedidiah answered, "I wanted Ayita to have the opportunity to see her father and mother again. "I also wanted to meet her family."

Her father said, "Jedidiah, although you are small in stature, you have a big heart."

Around the fire that evening, Ayita's father told them that he had heard there was a wagon train forming in Ft. Smith, Arkansas, which would be traveling to Santa Fe. They would be passing a day and a half, and ride south of the village in a few days. They could meet the wagon train at a place known as Childers Station. It would be easier and perhaps better for them if they travelled by wagon train. Her father told them that he would go with them to Childers Station and talk to them.

Ayita's mother was happy to see her daughter again. She had feared she would never know of her fate after she had left with Buffalo Bill Cody. At first, Ayita's parents were not sure about the little man she belonged to, but soon they learned to like him. Ayita had told them about Jedidiah tracking down the four men who had killed his sister. She also told them about his shooting ability and that she trusted him enough to allow him to shoot targets out of her hands. Others in the village, upon hearing these stories, wanted to see it for themselves. Ayita and Jedidiah set up a show for the village that evening around a large fire. She held a gourd in each hand, and he would shoot them. She hid behind her mother while Jedidiah got on Goliath. He came riding into the circle and Ayita stood up holding the gourds. As she held them up, he shot twice, destroying the gourds. Jedidiah told her later that night he only agreed to please her and show her family what they had done. He then told her he would never again point a weapon in her direction. He would continue to practice, but only for their protection.

The next morning, Ayita, Jedidiah, Ayita's father, and four young warriors from the village rode south to Childers Station. A little after noon of the second day, they came to the station. It was a large trading post with a mail drop inside. Its biggest claim was that it was a stop on the most southern route of the Santa Fe trail. At times, it was considered one of the more dangerous routes, since it crossed the Indian Territory. The wagon train operators had made deals with the different tribes telling them they would not take any more game than what they needed to eat along the way. They were not to kill or take any buffalo though. Jedidiah made camp behind the trading post to wait for the wagon train. The proprietor had told them that the train had not come past yet but was expected any day.

The wagon train arrived late in the afternoon and set up camp for the night. Jedidiah, Ayita, and her father went to speak to the wagon master. Once they introduced themselves to the wagon master Colonel Abrams he said, "I have heard of Jedidiah by reputation."

Ayita's father told Colonel Abrams, "I assure you, there will be no trouble through the nations."

Jedidiah said, "I have traveled across the plains alone."

Col. Abrams stated, "I agree to take the two of you along with the train. Jedidiah and Ayita, if anybody gives you any trouble, I will take care of it."

Jedidiah told him, "I can help with scouting and hunting for food.

Abrams said, "we are allowed to kill what they needed to eat, but no buffalo–at least not till they reached Texas." Abrams then said, "they could tie their mule behind his wagon."

Jedidiah told him that he had learned of a few places and ways to find some water. The wagon master said that each wagon carried two barrels of fresh water which should last them across to the mountains. They wouldn't have any trouble finding water till they got into far western Oklahoma Territory. The couple moved their camp in with the wagon train for the night. Ayita's father stayed the night with them and talked more with the wagon master.

At dawn, the wagon train started moving west. Jedidiah and Ayita rode on Goliath alongside Abram's wagon. The first three days went well and there was no trouble. On the fourth day, they saw some Indians near the train and a few of the people were scared. Jedidiah and

Ayita rode out to talk to the Indians, and they rode away after. That night, some of the people accused Ayita of consorting with the Indians. She told them that she had talked to them about the trail and the rivers, asking if it was good to pass. They told her that it was a good season for travel. They had heard of the train, and they were to let it pass. She told the people of the wagon train that the warriors were Chickasaw, and they would cause no trouble with the wagon train.

One of the men started to protest about Ayita on the train. Colonel Abrams shut him up and told him that Ayita would protect them more than anything else they could have while in the nations. Later, Jedidiah asked Abrams what he meant by that. Colonel Abrams asked him if he didn't know who his wife was. Seeing a puzzled look on his face, Abrams went on to explain that her father was a major leader of the Cherokee nation and envoy amongst many of the other tribes. Jedidiah said he knew she was a princess but assumed that was just his opinion of her.

The trip went pretty smoothly till they reached the western part of the territory. Many times, they had seen a few Indians ride near the train and watch for an hour or so. This time, a large band rode alongside about a quarter mile away. These Indians looked fierce. Watching them for a few minutes, Jedidiah and Ayita confirmed they were Comanche. Jedidiah rode up to the colonel and asked if Abrams had approved of him riding out to the warriors to talk to them. He knew a few Comanche and a leader, so he might be able to talk with them.

Jedidiah and Ayita rode out to the warriors. They all stopped and watched with their eyes wide open. Jedidiah addressed them with the few Comanche words he had learned. The one in front told him he spoke English. The leader then looked at Ayita, asking her name. She told him who she was and he in turn told the rest. The leader then looked at Jedidiah and Goliath. He said that he had heard of him and how he had taken on the Robbers Roost single handed. He also said he had heard of the mighty warrior who was very small and rode a giant horse. That this man was very fast and accurate with his gun. Jedidiah told him that he was that man and that he and his wife were going to the New Mexico territory to build a home and start a new life there. The warrior told him that he and his wagons could go in peace. He also told them that he was a warrior and that Ayita was one of them. If they needed meat, they could take what they needed. The leader whooped loudly, and the Comanche warriors all turned and rode away.

Jedidiah and Ayita rode back to Colonel Abrams and told him what had been said. That night around the campfire, Abrams told the entire train members how Ayita and Jedidiah had helped them. Colonel Abrams then told the camp that if Ayita had not been with them, they might have had a much harder time going through the nations. Her father was a major leader amongst the Cherokee and often consulted with all the tribes of the Indian Territory. Ayita herself was a Princess of the Cherokee people. He then told them that they would soon be going into land with little water. They should each make sure to fill their barrels of water every time they stopped at a water source. They may have to go for several days at a time without finding any fresh water. At best traveling speed for a wagon train, they were a month away from Santa Fe. Days before they reached Las Vegas they would find a good river with plenty of water. That was over three weeks away. Every day, water would get harder and harder to find.

Nobody on the train gave Jedidiah or Ayita any trouble after the Comanche sighting. Once they left the Oklahoma Territory and went into the Texas panhandle, water was scarce. They often went for three or four days before finding fresh water. At least once they were only able to fill half of their barrels. One morning after they had gone four days without finding water, Jedidiah was riding on the forward left flank and topped a low hill. He stopped to look around as he often would do. Far to the south, he was sure that he could see a line of trees. If so, this could indicate a river or at least a creek. He asked Ayita to walk down to the train and catch up with Abrams. He wanted her to tell him that he was going to ride in that direction to look for water. While he was talking with Ayita, he gave Goliath a good drink of water from his canteen.

Ayita walked fast to Abrams and told him what Jedidiah had seen and what he was scouting for. Colonel Abrams told the members of the train to slow down and for everyone but the drivers to walk. Jedidiah pushed Goliath at a fast cant toward the dark line on the horizon. It took him just over two hours to get to it, but long before, he could tell that he was seeing trees. Soon he came upon a running stream of fresh water coming from the west. He turned Goliath northwest to intercept the wagon train. When he caught up with the train, he told Abrams about the stream and the train turned towards it.

A little after the sun sat behind the western horizon they came to the stream. The wagon train circled on a rise above the stream at the edge of the few trees along the bank. They were able to get their fill of water and collect wood for campfires. The men took turns through the night watching and listening for possible trouble. They were in Kiowa and Apache territory now, along with a few wild Comanche. Colonel Abrams chose to stay two nights here and allow everyone to get plenty of water. When they left, it would be six days before they found water again. This time, it took all night for them to fill their barrels.

Sixteen days after leaving the Oklahoma Territory, they came to a valley with a flowing river. The water looked muddy but was drinkable. By this time, they were not fussy about it being a little dirty. They soon learned that once the water was in the barrel, the dirt settled to the bottom, leaving cleaner water on top to drink. Abrams told them this was the Canadian River and since they had arrived at it early in the afternoon, they would leave at first light. It would take two and a half days to get to Las Vegas if they went straight through the mesa. They may find a limited amount of water in catches in the hills. If they went around the mesa, there would be no water, and it would take a day longer. He would take the longer route as wandering through the mesa could be rough traveling.

The next night they stopped with a dry camp. Abrams had warned the people to use their water sparingly and to give their stock water first. On the second morning going around the mesa, they saw Indians riding on either side of them. Jedidiah rode up to the front of the train after letting Ayita off to walk. He told Abram that he would try something. He rode out in front of the train about a hundred yards. He had baffled the Apache before with his size and the size of his horse. He was hoping that it would work again. If not, he and many of the men were well armed. Colonel Abrams kept the train moving at the same pace as Jedidiah. He knew that if they were just curious, they would follow a while then move on. If something or someone had stirred them up, though, they would attack. Abrams was ready to have the train circle the wagons at a moment's notice. Two of the warriors rode closer to Jedidiah and looked right at him, then rode away at a fast pace. They went to another up on the hill. Soon, all the Apache rode away.

That evening, Abrams looked for a camp site up on a hill with a good view. He found such a place with a rocky escarpment in the center. He circled the wagons around the escarpment to make camp for the night and assigned two men to stand guard at the top. They would be relieved every two hours. Jedidiah and Ayita took one of the watches early in the morning hours. They sat on top of the hill twenty feet above the top of the wagon's white canvas tops. They sat back-to-back and slowly scanned the horizon. They used their peripheral vision to observe the closer shrubs for movement. They dared not whisper to each other so as not to give away their position. Jedidiah took her hand and held it till they were relieved.

Three more days went by without anybody seeing the Apache. By midafternoon they came into Las Vegas. Jedidiah got a room for him and Ayita in the hotel he had stayed at before. He placed Goliath and the mule in the stable, paying extra for good care of both of them. Abrams told them all that they would move out at first light the next morning. He told them that they were a little over three days from Santa Fe. There would be water all along the way for them. They would stay two nights in Santa Fe before moving on west toward California.

Three days later in the afternoon, the wagon train rolled into Santa Fe, New Mexico Territory. Jedidiah and Ayita thanked Colonel Abrams and said goodbye. They placed their stock in a livery stable and checked into the hotel. It was the same hotel Jedidiah had stayed at before and the staff remembered him. Before dark, Jedidiah and Ayita walked along main street looking for property they could buy. The sheriff walked up to them and recognized Jedidiah. He asked them what they had in mind. Jedidiah told him they were looking to settle there and open a business. He told them they would be welcomed and after hearing what they had in mind, he told them that there was a vacant lot not far from the sheriff's office for a reasonable price. If they were interested, he would introduce them to the owner tomorrow morning.

Chapter 16: Home

On their first morning in Santa Fe, Jedidiah took Ayita to the restaurant across the street and down a short distance from the hotel. They had a quiet evening before returning to their hotel room. Shortly after they returned to their room, they heard a knock at the door. Sheriff Andrew and another man stood at the door. Andrew introduced Clay, the owner of the lot that was for sale. They came to a deal for the land and Andrew told them where they could buy the lumber and find help building. Jedidiah and Ayita told him they wanted to build a store with their home above on the second floor. They wanted a balcony on the second floor looking over the street. The lot was on the west side of the street so they could get the morning sun and have some wind block during the winter months.

Over the next few days Jedidiah and Ayita talked to a local man about helping to build the store. Together, they decided to build an adobe structure. Gomez had many adobe bricks already made through the sunbaked method. After Ayita told him she wanted a kiln for pottery behind the store, he suggested he build it first and use it to bake bricks for the construction. It would greatly speed up the process. Jedidiah offered to help bring in the clay, sand, and grass they would need, once Gomez showed him where to get it. Jedidiah and Ayita drew up a rough plan for what they wanted. Gomez was sure he could help them build it. He had sons and nephews who would help with the work. They reached an agreement and construction started. There would be a fireplace in the store large enough for Ayita to bake some smaller pieces. There was also a fireplace on the second floor for heating and cooking. Just outside the back door on the right was the large kiln for making pottery.

Jedidiah and Ayita went to the place that Gomez showed them to load clay. They had bought a small wagon and hitched Goliath to it. Ayita checked out the clay and found some that would work for her pottery. They loaded a large amount and took it back to the store. Most of it went to the pile that Gomez and his family were using to make the adobe. Later, they went and brought in the other materials needed for the construction. The store began going up right next to the restaurant. Jedidiah and Ayita became regulars in the restaurant, and the owners were eager for them to open the new store next to them.

In the evenings, Ayita painted. She had picked up a few supplies for this hobby in Paris and brought it back. These would be some of the first things she would display for sale in the store once it was open. Jedidiah was asked to work in the sheriff's office one day to repair their guns. Other than a few odd jobs for new friends, they worked most of the time building the store and their new home.

One day, two months later, the owner of the hotel asked Ayita about all the paintings she had. She told him she was painting them and would place them in the store once it was built. The owner asked if she would mind placing them on the wall in the hotel lobby. She could even put prices on them and if they were sold, she could collect and place another up. She agreed. The hotel placed six of her paintings on the walls in the lobby. At least once a week after that one or more would sell.

One day two men rode into town with three wagons following. Jedidiah was working inside the store, which was not even half finished. He looked up to see the men and walked outside to get a closer look. Recognizing one, he yelled, "William, it's Jedidiah."

William Bonney spoke to the other man before walking over to Jedidiah. They shook hands, smiling and laughing. The other man walked over, and Billy the Kid introduced Jedidiah to John Tunstall. They all went into the restaurant for a cup of coffee and Jedidiah told them all about Europe and the Wild West Show. While he was talking to them, Ayita came in looking for him. He introduced his wife to Billy the Kid and John Tunstall. John told him that they were going south where he intended to start a ranch. He had met William in Las Vegas and talked him into going to work for him. John said that William was a good boy at heart and just needed a chance. They rode out of Santa Fe the next day going to Lincoln County.

Days of working on the store and house changed into weeks and then months. Ayita started to show… they would be having a child. Jedidiah couldn't be prouder, yet he worried. Would the child be small like him or beautiful like Ayita? He wished with all his heart that any child they may have would look like her. Each day, he told her that too. Ayita had learned to appreciate this show of affection from her husband. It pleased her to hear such caring words from Jedidiah. She thought back to when her father had made a deal with Buffalo Bill Cody for her. He had told her that he wanted her to see the white man's world and have a better chance in life. He had predicted that she would have a great adventure and see many wondrous things. Buffalo Bill never treated her badly. She was a daughter to him. Ayita had expected to be his woman, but he was always fatherly to her. When she met Jedidiah, she saw kindness and love in his eyes. Even with his tenderness, she also saw the toughness of a warrior. After the many walks and meals, they shared, she was happy when he asked her to marry him. Soon, she would give him a child. She hoped he would be a son. What man didn't want a son to help him and learn from him?

It took four months for the building to be finished. They were beginning to wonder if they would be in their home before the baby was born. Jedidiah had started pushing Gomez and himself while working on the building. In the end, they did finish before the big event, and the couple was able to move into their new home before the baby was born. Together, they opened the store on a Monday morning. The right side of the store was pottery and art. On the left side were guns and a desk for gun repair and making of ammunition. Covering every wall were the pictures they had bought from all over the east and Europe where they had traveled. Stepping into the store, a person was able to travel with them through their pictures. You could follow from their first show to their last show with the Buffalo Bill Cody Wild West Show. On the right-side Ayita's paintings hung, and on the counters, her pottery sat. On the left side there was a showcase for handguns. Behind the case was a raised platform on which Jedidiah could stand and walk along, bringing him eye to eye with the customers.

Jedidiah had learned a trick that he brought to his gunsmith store. He left the firing pin out of every gun. Only after the sale and money put away did he put the firing pin back in. He also always wore his gun. William Bonney once told him, "When you're as fast as you are, there will always be someone wanting to try you."

Besides fixing and maintaining guns, he had a good supply of new guns for sale. He had ordered and been receiving them for some time now. He had the new Winchester 73 rifle which was greatly sought after. Santa Fe was planning a big celebration and asked him if he could get a special rifle for them to give away as the prize. Jedidiah had sent a special request and was waiting for the reply. While waiting, John Chisum came into the store to order a special rifle for himself. He ordered a hand-crafted rifle and two cases of Winchester 73's for his hands. He also ordered two thousand rounds of ammunition. Once that order had been sent via telegraph, he received word that a special rifle was being sent for the city's event. It was what they were calling one in one thousand.

Jedidiah talked to the mayor of Santa Fe, telling him that he was going to receive a special rifle for their event. The mayor invited him to the next city council meeting.

As they were talking, Ayita stated, "It is time," and started walking toward the stairs up to their home.

As Jedidiah moved the help her the mayor said, "I will go get the doctor"

Hours later, Ayita gave birth to a healthy baby boy. Jedidiah asked the doctor, "is he normal?"

Smiling, the doctor said, "There is no signs of dwarfism in the child."

Jedidiah then asked, "is Ayita okay?"

The doctor stated, "she is fine and will be able to get up and around in a few hours."

A week later, Jedidiah went to the city council meeting. Once there, they discussed the year coming up as being the United States Centennial. The city was planning a big celebration with games and shows all week long. The mayor then recognized Jedidiah and asked about the grand prize. He told them that Winchester had agreed to send him a special model 1873 they called One in One Thousand. He had received a letter describing it as the perfect rifle–one that was exceptionally handcrafted, and gold plated. It was one that every piece fitted perfectly and was the smoothest action of any they made. They wouldn't sell it but sent it out as a singular token. He then told them that he thought that it was a large sale to John Chisum that had secured the prize rifle for his store. The council told him that they would have a turkey shoot with the best gunmen in the territory trying for the rifle.

Smiling, Jedidiah said, "I guess it wouldn't be fair if I entered so I'll abstain from the competition."

One of the council members told Jedidiah that he was thinking of moving to California and suggested that he run for his position. Jedidiah told him he would think about it and talk to his wife.

Six months later, a freight wagon came with two guards. The wagon went to the Wells Fargo office and soon the two guards followed with a man carrying a box to Jedidiah's gun shop. The sheriff saw the procession and walked over to the gunsmith. They all entered and laid the box on top of the counter. Jedidiah looked at all of the men standing there, then picked up a hammer and pried open the box. Clearing the packing straw, he picked up the most beautiful rifle he had even seen. "Wow, One in One Thousand. This gun is worth more than every gun I have in this store," Jedidiah exclaimed.

By that time, the mayor had heard about the delivery and walked in to see. "We have to spread the word throughout the territory about this rifle and the contest," the mayor said. "The more men we get here and pay to try for this gun, the more money we will make. It could be the busiest week this town has ever had."

Aside from the turkey shoot, they talked about having games, shows, and entertainment on the streets. They began plans for a horse race starting and ending on main street. One of the council men looked at Jedidiah and asked if he would be willing to put on a gun shooting exhibition, since he wouldn't compete in the turkey shoot. He told them he had an idea for the turkey shoot of placing an axle just below a curtain. They could place targets at different intervals around the axle and have it turned from the side. This would have the target spin and pop up from behind the curtain. They would be able to move the shooters back after each round or speed up the revolution of the axle.

"Before the competition starts," Jedidiah said, "I can shoot from the maximum range at the fastest speed with six targets on the axle."

A council man asked, "Can you hit all six like that?"

Jedidiah smiled and said, "It wouldn't be a problem."

Jedidiah and Ayita's store was getting popular. People came in just to look at the pictures. Some people bought a painting or piece of pottery from them while some would leave a gun to be repaired. Jedidiah sold new guns on occasion. Late one afternoon, Jedidiah looked out onto the street to see several riders around four wagons. He recognized the man in front and went outside to greet him.

Wyatt Earp was leading his family, moving from Kansas to Tucson, Arizona. With them was Doc Holiday. As they rode into Santa Fe, Wyatt saw a little man walk out of a store toward him. He flipped the strap off the hammer of his gun. He never knew if someone might know of his reputation and be gunning for him. As the man walked into the sunlight, Wyatt recognized his friend.

He talked with Jedidiah for a few minutes and promised to visit him in the store once he had the family settled in for the night. Later, Wyatt, his brother Virgil, and Doc came into the store. They had Jedidiah work on their guns while they talked about their plans. They told Jedidiah that the train was coming this way and one day it would be in Santa Fe. Wyatt looked at all the pictures on the wall while Jedidiah replaced the firing pin on his colt. Wyatt told him that it looked like he and Ayita had a great adventure. Jedidiah told him it was interesting and fun to see all those places, but they were happy where they were now. The Earp brothers, along with Doc. Holiday, left Santa Fe at dawn the next morning, going west.

***

A stagecoach came into town at top speed and went straight to the jail. A little later, the sheriff came to the gun shop to talk to Jedidiah. He told him that the stage had been jobbed, and the men went up into the mountains. The sheriff was forming a posse to ride after the men. He wanted Jedidiah to stay in town and be deputized to maintain law over the town while he and his deputy were gone. He wanted someone good with a gun he could trust in case the outlaws came to town while he was away. He told Jedidiah that there were two men both heavy set and medium height. He explained that there were many bad men around Lincoln County and some of them may be up here, the likes of Jess Evans and Billy the Kid. Jedidiah reminded him that he knew Billy the Kid and he hoped that he didn't have anything to do with the robbery.

Jedidiah talked to Ayita after the sheriff had left. He told her that if she needed him, he would be around, but he would be at the jail or on the street most of the time. He would look in on her every chance he could. He walked the streets just like he had seen the sheriff do many times. The banker greeted him as he went past. Three days went by with Jedidiah watching over Santa Fe. There were no problems except two young boys fist fighting in an alley. He broke up the fight and sent them home to their parents. The posse came back to town without having found the outlaws. They had lost the trail up on the mountain.

A week went by with no information about the robbers. The next stage came through with a message that they had been caught in Mora two days after the sheriff had lost their trail up on the mountain.

The week of the centennial came, and the town filled with people. The cantina set up a wagon with beer barrels on the street selling beer right off the wagon. Sixty men signed up for the turkey shot to try for the rifle. The mayor stood on a platform and announced. "Before the competition starts, the world-renowned 'Little Gun' from the Buffalo Bill Cody Wild West Show is going to give us a shooting exhibition!"

Jedidiah stood at the far mark and nodded his head. The axle turned, popping up the targets at a fast pass. All six targets were destroyed by the end of a full turn of the device.

A voice came from the back of the crowd saying, "I would like to match that." William Bonney walked up smiling at Jedidiah. Ayita was standing nearby and gasped in fear. She was afraid Billy the Kid would draw on Jedidiah.

The two men shook hands and Jedidiah loudly proclaimed, "I have an idea." He called for the man operating the wheel turning the targets to place twelve targets on the axle. "Let's scatter six red and six blue around." Jedidiah allowed Billy the Kid to choose his color, and he picked red.

Jedidiah told the onlookers that he and Billy would stand side by side and whoever shot all his colored targets first was the winner. The mayor was to signal for the wheel to begin turning.

As the targets popped up, they both fired their guns. Jedidiah placed his gun back in his holster as Billy fired his last shot. They both had knocked out all of their targets, but

Jedidiah was slightly faster. Billy told him that he had gotten even faster than he had been when they had last met.

The celebration continued all week, as did the turkey shoot. On the last day, the shoot was down to two men. After backing them out to three hundred yards and spinning the target at top speed, a buffalo hunter won. He came to the platform to collect his new rifle and was introduced to the crowd as Pat Garratt.

After the centennial celebration, the town slowly quieted down. A normal routine returned as did regular business. Jedidiah's gunsmith business improved, possibly due to his exhibition or his acquiring the Winchester rifle. He and Ayita received a letter from Buffalo Bill Cody. He was putting together another wild west show and invited them to be a part of it. Jedidiah looked at Ayita, and she shook her head. He smiled and wrote a letter back declining the offer, telling Buffalo Bill they had a son now and was already expecting another child.

***

Ayita gave birth to a perfectly normal baby girl. The newspaper was filled with stories about trouble in Lincoln County involving Jess Evans, Billy the Kid, John Tunstall, John Chisum and Lawerence Murphy. Santa Fe was busy with railroad workers. The train tracks had come from the east and Las Vegas and were going west. A large yard had been erected along the tracks to store large amounts of rail, cross timbers, and material for the construction.

Months later in February, the paper posted the story that John Tunstall had been killed. The news and the stories told by travelers were conflicting as to what the people who knew John believed. The paper and official word was that John had pulled a gun on deputies. Anyone who knew John Tunstall would not believe it as he never carried a gun and would have nothing to do with one. By spring, Ayita told Jedidiah that she was with child again. They now had a three-year-old son and almost one year old girl. Jedidiah was proud as any father could be.

A new story in the paper later called the conflict down south the Lincoln County War. It named a few men who had been killed and stock that had been stolen. A few days later, the paper stated on the front page that Billy the Kid was wanted for the murder of the sheriff in Lincoln County and his deputies. As Jedidiah and Ayita were reading the story in their store, they looked up as the door opened, and the sheriff came in. Ayita took the children and went upstairs to the living quarters.

The sheriff said to Jedidiah, "I know that Billy and you are friends. It was reported that Billy and the regulators were in the area. I am going out after them and would like you to go along with me and the posse. Perhaps with you along with us, we can bring him in alive."

Jedidiah told him he would get his things and say goodbye to Ayita. Then he would go saddle his mountain horse. Jedidiah had purchased a small mountain mustang that had the stamina and sure footedness for this country. He joined the sheriff and a large posse in the street. Jedidiah rode up front next to the sheriff. As they rode, the sheriff told him that there was a large shipment of cash coming in on the next train which was supposed to be shipped to the Murphy Bank in Lincoln County. It was expected that Billy the Kid might try to take that shipment.

The sheriff's posse found no evidence of men trying to stop the train. The train, along with the money, made it into Santa Fe and four guards loaded it onto the stage to Lincoln. An army patrol had come to town to escort the stage to the bank. Once they pulled out of Santa Fe, it was out of the sheriffs' hands. Jedidiah went to the store and told Ayita all about their long peaceful ride.

Ayita and Jedidiah talked about their house. It was nice but was becoming small with a third child on the way. They had only used half of their money to build the store and house and had invested the other half in the bank here in Santa Fe. They had done well in business at the store and invested much of the profits. They went for a ride that morning to look for a place to build a new home. At the eastern edge of the town, they found a perfect place. Jedidiah was concerned, though, as he saw no water close by. Ayita pointed to the trees and a greener spot at the point that a ravine started. They led their horses to the spot, and the horses began sniffing at the ground. Jedidiah dug down a short distance and water seeped into the hole.

"We can dig a well here and build a large house on the rise above," Jedidiah said.

Their new home was built over the next five months. It was a large estate made of adobe. It looked like many of the rancheros in the area. Once the house itself was completed, they had an adobe wall built around the house and the well. A veranda overlooked the growing city. A boy was born who was normal as the other two had been. Jedidiah and Ayita had a carriage which they used Goliath to pull. Each morning, they loaded the family onto the carriage and went to the store. The children played under the watchful eyes of their loving parents.

Jedidiah ran for city council and was elected by an overwhelming majority. He was home and lived a happy life with his family.

The End

About the Author

Terry Godfrey is an author from Binger, OK and is a member of the Oklahoma Writers Federation, Inc. He has published multiple books, many of which are located in Binger and southwestern Oklahoma. He writes across several genres, including science fiction, historical fiction, murder mysteries, young adult, and romance. He has also written newspaper articles as a freelance journalist. Terry has helped other first-time authors publish their books.

Book Titles

A Tough Row to Hoe	10-3-2018
The Day the Earth Stopped	12-9-2018
To Run With the Big Dogs	12-19-2018
Bitsy's First Deer Season	1-21-2019
Murder at Medicine Creek	1-24-2019
[pen name TDG]	
Legend of Indian Head Rock	7-9-2019
Skyfish	7-24-2019
Love Across the Creek	3-15-2021
Voyage to One Helluva Day	7-19-2023
Society of Mars Exploration I	8-10-2023
Society of Mars Exploration II	8-10-2023
Society of Mars Exploration III	8-11-2023
Society of Mars Exploration IV	8-10-2023
Society of Mars Exploration	3-7-2024
(the complete series hardback)	
Murder by a Flower [pen name TDG]	3-12-2024
Love Under the Leg Lamp	7-1-2024
[pen name Teri G]	
Empress and the Cyberginics	1-8-2025
*Success with Direct Sales	1-19-2025
Nowhere to Die	3-24-2025

* 2025 nonfiction published contest finalist at WritersCon